RISING TO THE CALL

Rosie Mather is captivated by the ideals of the women who are prepared to fight for their right to vote — but Sam Hardshaw, the young man in her life, has more conservative views and wants his woman to submissively take her place in the home. Forced to choose between the man she loves or 'rising to the call' of the Suffragists, Rosie makes her choice. Will their love find a way to surmount the difficulties her decision brings?

Books by Karen Abbott
in the Linford Romance Library:

RED ROSE GIRL
SUMMER ISLAND
A TIME TO FORGIVE
LOVE IS BLIND
LOVE CONQUERS ALL
A MATTER OF TRUST
DESIGNS FOR LOVE
WHEN TRUE LOVE WINS
A TASTE OF HAPPINESS
THE HEART KNOWS NO BOUNDS
THE TURNING TIDE
OUTRAGEOUS DECEPTION

KAREN ABBOTT

RISING TO THE CALL

Complete and Unabridged

LINFORD
Leicester

First published in Great Britain in 2004

First Linford Edition
published 2005

British Library CIP Data

Abbott, Karen
Rising to the call.—Large print ed.—
Linford romance library
1. Women—Suffrage—Great Britain—Fiction
2. Love stories
3. Large type books
I. Title
823.9′2 [F]

ISBN 1–84395–693–4

Published by
F. A. Thorpe (Publishing)
Anstey, Leicestershire

Set by Words & Graphics Ltd.
Anstey, Leicestershire
Printed and bound in Great Britain by
T. J. International Ltd., Padstow, Cornwall

This book is printed on acid-free paper

1

The afternoon light was fading fast. An early-evening mist was already drifting across the streets of Bolton, leaving a wispy trail over the silvered ground. The lamplighter made his way methodically along the pavements. The yellow glow in each lamp fluttered into life and stretched out behind him like a string of pale amber.

The figure of a young woman hurried along the street behind him, the smart clicking of her heeled boots echoing into the gloom. Her dark hair was swept up into a large coil on the top of her head. A wide scarf held her hat in place and served to keep out some of the cold. As the mist coiled around her, she hugged her clothes tighter to her body. They were more serviceable than fashionable, bought from the market and made to fit with skilful cutting. On her trim figure, anything looked good, so what did it matter if her clothes were mended and more out of date than she cared to think about?

She pulled the wide lapels of her coat across her chest and adjusted her muffler around the lower part of her face. Only her shining eyes betrayed her excitement. If she hurried, she'd catch the next tram and be home before her father and her brother. She could even have their tea ready for when they came in. She'd light the gas-lamps and put a piece of holly, saved from their Christmas festivities, into the bread and butter pudding and when they asked her if she was sure they could afford to have a pudding, she'd tell them her surprise. She couldn't wait to see their faces, and her dad would smile at her across the table and say . . .

'A job? What does tha mean, got a job? Tha doesn't need a job! Tha's got one 'ere, takin' care of us!'

It was her brother, Fred Mather, who spoke first, glancing around the table, looking for, and receiving, approving nods of agreement from his father. The delighted smile wavered on Rosie's face. This wasn't how she had planned it. She'd wanted them to be pleased. She'd thought they would congratulate her and say how wonderful it was that it would help no end.

'The interview was this afternoon,' she added, her voice faltering a little. 'I'm to be an assistant librarian at the library in town.'

'What?' Fred asked, his voice slightly higher-pitched than usual in his evident surprise.

Rosie felt the first stirrings of anxiety.

'I've got a job as an assistant librarian,' she repeated. 'I was ever so nervous. I was the only girl being interviewed. I didn't think I'd get it but I did well on the test.'

She knew she was babbling. She always babbled when she was nervous. It was one of her major sources of embarrassment.

'I start on Monday, ten shillings a

week. I know it's not much but . . .'

'Well, you'll 'ave to go back and tell them you've changed your mind, won't you? We need you here. Who's going to make our tea if you're out gallivantin' in town? And all t'washin' and t'cleanin' and such!'

Fred's tone was adamant, brooking no argument, but Rosie faced him angrily. She might have known that Fred would stand against her. He was a firm union man and didn't like to think women could do a worthwhile job.

'I've got the job on my merit and will be just as good, if not better, than any man you might care to name!'

'No-one has said you couldn't, love,' Alf's voice broke in, 'but Fred's right. We need you here!'

He resumed his eating of the stew she had left cooking slowly in the fire oven whilst she'd been out, showing that he considered the matter to be settled. Rosie pressed her lips together and glared, first at her dad and then at her brother. Her eyes narrowed slightly as she watched him calmly put the next spoonful of stew into his mouth.

'Well, if all you want is a skivvy for a sister, Fred Mather, you can think again! I'm not content to simply clean and cook for the rest of my life. You'd better marry your precious Edith and get her to become your slave!'

Fred banged his fist on to the table.

'I'll marry Edith when I'm good and ready, so keep your nose out of it! At least she'll do as she's told, not like you!'

'Well, you've got that bit right!'

Rosie faced him angrily, refusing to back down, even though she knew her brother's temper and had caught the backside of it many a time in her nineteen years.

Alf picked up the last piece of bread and wiped it around his dish. After he had pushed it into his mouth, he pushed his dish away from him. His face was lined and his eyes saddened, and not only because he was still mourning the loss of his wife. Three months ago, Dolly's lungs had finally given up on the unequal task of battling with the millions of fine shreds of cotton that floated in the air of the carding room at the mill at the bottom of their street. Then, a month later, a devastating, crippling accident had befallen him. A greasy patch on the engine-shed floor had gone unseen. The first he had known was when his legs whooshed from under him and a shattering pain shot through his back as he landed on the sharp edge of the cast-iron bogie he had been working on.

'Not paying attention', was the cold opinion of the management, refusing to be held liable for the accident.

Their gift of a few pounds to tide him over was magnanimously given, along with the disclaimer of responsibility. Everyone knew he would never walk, or work, again. He now shook his head in tired resignation.

'Anyway, lass, a librarian! We're working-class, Rosie, and nowt else!'

He flapped his arms helplessly at his sides.

'Get me up! I needs me old pipe!' he ordered impatiently.

He was as helpless as a baby, and it near broke his heart. Coming just after he had lost his beloved wife, it was a double blow that everyone who knew him never expected him to recover from, but he had, though he hated every reminder of his disability. Fred and Rosie leaped to do his bidding and Rosie waited until they had settled Alf into the worn armchair by the fireside.

'No-one has to stay working-class, Dad! I want to use my brains, not work my fingers to the bone or get my lungs full of smoke and cotton fluff like most folks around here! You know that was what Mam wanted!'

If she had thought that the reference to her mother's dreams for her would persuade Alf to her way of thinking she was mistaken.

'Yer mam didn't want you dashing down to the mill every morning, like t'lasses we hear at six o'clock! Be thankful I am keeping to her wishes!'

'But, Dad!'

Fred scowled as Rosie's mouth set in a stubborn line.

'And watch how you speak to our dad! It's no use looking like that,' he warned her. 'You've had your answer and that's that!'

Rosie scowled back at him. She supposed she'd known how they'd feel, really. That was why she hadn't told them about the job before the interview.

'I'm not giving in,' she challenged Fred, tilting her chin up proudly. 'We can't manage on the money you're bringing in. I've got to do something!'

'What d'you mean, we can't manage? We're doing all right, aren't we?'

Fred glanced around the back kitchen, which was where they cooked, ate and spent most of their leisure time. There was the table and four wooden chairs. Alf's old armchair had seen better days and there was also a misshapen sofa, adorned with a number of bright cushions, whose fabric matched the two mid-length curtains now drawn across the window.

There were two cupboards, one for their food and the other for their meagre amount of pots and pans. A number of rugs were scattered on the floor, and a few embers glowed in the small grate, which served both as their means of keeping warm and their means of cooking.

There was a small, front room. It used to be grandly known as the sitting-room, though it, too, was sparsely furnished with an elderly sofa, two chairs and a polished table of uncertain age, used more in the summer when no fuel was required to keep the room warm. Rosie's mam had been proud of her sitting-room and Rosie had intended to keep it spotless in her memory, but now, since his accident, Alf's bed was in there.

Upstairs wasn't much better. There were two bedrooms but the back bedroom had been divided into two, to accommodate Fred and Rosie. Rosie's room was hardly larger than the narrow bed that was in it but Fred's section was larger. Fred had recently moved into the larger front room. Rosie wondered if he was thinking of marrying Edith Fisher, his girl friend, and intending to welcome her into the Mather home.

That would mean four mouths to feed, and more, perhaps, as time went on. Edie had already confided in Rosie that all she wanted from life was a husband and lots of babies. Though not overjoyed by the prospect of Edie living with them, goodness knows how she would manage to cope with her dad on her own if Fred moved out.

'If you're not managing on the money I give you, you should organise yourself better. Buy cheaper cuts of meat or something. Mam always managed!' Fred now reminded her.

Rosie shook her head in exasperation.

'Dad was working then. We had more than double what we've got now.'

She cast a glance over to where Alf was sitting, his eyes staring unseeingly at the fire. She could tell at a glance her words had upset him and dropped on to her knees at his feet, taking his calloused hand in hers.

'I'm sorry to upset you like this, Dad. I'm not blaming you. You can't help it, but we have to face the facts. Don't you see?'

She turned to look up at Fred.

'You've no idea, have you? I already buy the cheapest cuts. I wait until late in the afternoon, so that I can buy what's left over at the butcher's. He thinks we have a pet dog and he sometimes gives me extra scraps. It's the same at the greengrocer's and the bakery. Do you never wonder why we have stews all the time?'

Rosie looked down at the floor, not wanting to see the bleakness in their dad's eyes. She hadn't wanted to tell him or Fred how tight things were.

Although she didn't agree with her brother's strong views, she knew they weren't very different from those held by most of their neighbours. It was a man's world, and women were brought up to do as they were told.

'I do what I can,' she went on quietly, 'but I don't know how I can keep on managing.'

She stepped away from her dad and took an old pottery jug from the mantelpiece.

'It's almost empty. Most of Fred's money only covers a week's rent. The rest won't buy enough food to feed us all, never mind the doctor's fees.'

She grimaced slightly as she spoke the last few words, knowing Alf found it hard enough to bear not being able to work, without the doctor's fees being a constant drain on their limited amount of money.

'Well, we'll have to use some of Dad's compensation money, just to tide us over,' Fred declared. 'You got a few pounds, didn't you, Dad?'

He looked pleased with himself for thinking of the obvious solution. His satisfied grin faded as he took in Rosie's defeated expression.

'Why not? What's up wi' it?' he insisted.

Rosie looked at their dad, at the crushed look on Alf's face.

'It's all gone, on the rent, our food, our clothes.'

Her voice faded away to no more than a whisper.

'I'm sorry. There's none of it left.'

She saw Alf's body sag into his chair as he took in her words. The hopeless expression on Fred's face cut to her heart. She forced a bright smile on to her face.

'So, you see why I need a job, don't you? And it doesn't matter,' she quickly assured them. 'I'll enjoy it. Really, I will!'

That was true, she thought to herself. She longed to be back out in the world, instead of being cooped up in the house all day.

Fred turned away.

'It matters to me. How d'you think I feel? What sort of man am I, if I can't look after you and Dad?'

He'd been proud of his job at the locomotive works. He was a boiler-maker, a well-paid worker, until his hours had been reduced. Still, it was better than being laid off altogether.

'I know it upsets you,' Rosie said quietly, reaching out to touch her brother's hand but he jerked away from her. 'We have to face reality.'

Also, they must understand that a new world was emerging, Rosie thought, and it wasn't going to be purely a man's world for much longer. Women were determined to have their share. More and more of them were actively pursuing a greater say in their lives, no longer content to be the little woman at home, or pushed into a menial job with low pay and no rights.

In her eagerness to rally them to her own conviction, she almost took the argument into deeper waters. The suffragette movement had already seized her attention and ideas were growing within her, but not yet ready to be openly expressed. She hesitated.

Fred watched her thoughts flicker across her face. She had always been strong-headed, wilful, even, if the truth be told. Should have been a lad, she should. She got into as much trouble as one! Only their gentle mam had been able to sway her into more ladylike pursuits, and now she was gone. He was toying with the idea of asking Edie to marry him and she could come and look after him and their dad. Edie wouldn't be chasing after a job. She'd be right glad to give up the one she'd got and take on the two Mather men. She'd already said so, but not whilst Rosie still lived at home!

'Rosie'd make mincemeat out of me, she would!' Edie had declared, adding that she wouldn't share a kitchen with a hoyden like Rosie!

There was still the matter of money, though. His wage on short time simply wasn't enough. You needed at least two men to be out working in these hard times, and even that brought in only enough to barely exist on. Was Rosie right? Would Mam have wanted her to work in a library? It sounded genteel and their Rosie had the brains for it, no doubt about that.

Rosie was watching him closely.

'Just think of all those books I'd be working amongst. Shelves and shelves of them. It would be like heaven.'

Her face was alight, and Fred's expression softened slightly. He was losing the battle. Still, he didn't have to give in immediately, did he? He narrowed his eyes, watching her face.

'And who will see to all this?' he asked as he swung his hand around the room. 'And don't forget, Dad needs some looking after. You'll be out all day and too tired to do much when you get home. You needn't be thinking I'll be coming home and doing women's work!'

Rosie smiled.

'I've already had a word with Mrs Blackstock, next door. She said she'll be pleased to do for us for two shillings a week and it will only cost me a penny each way on the tram, so we'll still be seven shillings a week better off. That'll stretch your money such a lot further, won't it? And I'll be able to make our tea when I get home, or put it to cook slowly in the pot during the day. Dad can keep an eye on it, can't you, Dad? We'll still have to be careful, of course, but at least we won't starve, and I'll be able to get stuff cheap off Bolton market at the end of each day!'

Rosie smiled delightedly. She'd won! She knew it!

2

'Right, Miss Mather, if you will bring that selection of new books over to this table, you can show me how you intend to catalogue them. I don't want to have to stand over you all day long, making sure that you don't make any mistakes, nor do I want Mr Brown to have to keep going over your work.'

Mr Vermont glanced over to where one of the other assistant librarians was rearranging the Human Biology section. Four times a day they tidied the shelves to maintain the library's immaculate display.

Rosie staggered along behind the stooped figure of the senior librarian, to the designated table. The stack of books fitted neatly under her chin, a trick she had learned watching the other librarians.

'Right, here we are, Mr Vermont,' she

answered brightly.

His thin red lips pursed together, almost disappearing inside one another. The forefinger of his right hand shot to cover his pressed lips.

'Shush! Remember where we are!' he hissed.

'Sorry!' she mouthed silently at him. 'Shall I sit here?'

Her silent words were accompanied by elaborate gestures of her lips, her eyes dancing with merriment.

'Miss Mather, I would be obliged if you would treat this less frivolously!'

His indignation made his tone of voice rise sharply. Alarmed by the volume of his own voice, his eyes swivelled quickly from side to side. A few heads lifted and glanced in their direction, causing him to hunch his shoulders even more.

'Get on with it, Miss Mather,' he grated between his clenched lips.

'Certainly, Mr Vermont.'

Rosie pulled the cataloguing ledger towards her and efficiently entered the titles, class and code number of the varied books in front of her, thankful that she had always had a neat hand, as her school teachers had phrased it. Mr Vermont scrutinised her entries and could not find fault.

'Hmph! Not bad, Miss Mather,' he grunted.

Rosie realised that it was the nearest to a compliment she was to receive and smiled disarmingly. She was sure that somewhere underneath his bristling exterior there would be a heart of some sort but doubted if anyone had ever found it.

'Place those books in their correct positions on the shelves and work your way through the rest,' he commanded softly into her ear, preparing to take his leave of her. 'And be sure to move about silently.'

Shaking his head, his bent figure glided past the long rows of ceiling-high shelves, his hands clasped behind his back. Not a head stirred until his black-garbed presence had passed from sight.

Rosie got on with her work. She had been here for just over a week now and was thoroughly enjoying it. She felt vibrantly alive and in her natural element of books. She loved every one of them, whether they be large, much-handled, learned tomes, mainly for reference only, leather-bound classics, or some of the lighter, new, modern novels.

She rarely got away much before six o'clock in the evening, so it was always at least six-thirty by the time she got home, providing she didn't miss the tram. By thinking a day ahead of herself, she managed to have tea on the table for between seven to half-past, a bit later than her father was used to but she'd told him to have a bit of bread and cheese if he got hungry. She knew that Mrs Blackstock wouldn't let him go hungry, or short of a bit of company and conversation.

She was surprised by Fred's ready acceptance of his later-than-usual meal, until she realised that he liked the excuse to call in at the local pub with his pals on his way home from work and, she suspected, pursue his courtship of Edith Fisher, who lived at the far end of their street. No matter how poor they were, the men liked their pint, she would grumble to herself. Whatever the diversion, Fred seemed to time his arrival home with the moment she lifted the casserole dish out of the oven.

'Psst!'

Rosie jerked back to the present moment, and lifted her head in surprise and looked around quickly. Through a gap in the books on the shelf in front of her, a pair of laughing grey eyes met her glance.

'He's not bad once you get to know him!' the owner of the laughing eyes whispered.

She gestured with her hand towards the end of the bookshelf away from the central desk and moved off in that direction. She and Rosie met at the far end. She was a pretty young woman,

Rosie decided, probably in her early twenties. Her fair hair was swept up into a similar style to her own, though fastened into a tighter top-knot.

'More bark than bite, I think,' Rosie agreed quietly, reluctant to discuss her senior with others.

'He doesn't really like us women to be here,' the young woman continued. 'You'd think he'd be used to us by now. What's your name?'

'Rosie Mather, and you?'

'Annie Somers. I've been here nearly a year. I'm upstairs in the Ancient History department. I thought he would be bound to choose another man, so you could have knocked me down with a feather when I saw you come in last week! First job, is it?' she asked and Rosie nodded.

'Yes, and I'm so pleased to be working here. I'm hoping I'll be able to read some of these.'

She swept her arm around the thousands of books that filled the shelves.

'You can learn such a lot by reading, can't you? And there's so much I want to know!'

'Yes, it's time we women got our act together,' Annie commented, looking at Rosie thoughtfully. 'I don't know whether or not you've heard of the Women's Social and Political Union but, if you're interested, I'll take you along to one of our meetings.'

'Hush! Get on with your work, and less talking.'

It was Mr Vermont, his arms flapping wildly as he bore down upon them.

'Yes, Mr Vermont,' Annie agreed, and she swept a pile of books into her arms. 'I'll get in touch with you later,' she mouthed silently at Rosie.

Rosie felt her interest stirred. Annie struck a familiar chord with her. Wasn't the Women's Social and Political Union one of the women's suffragette movements? She had seen its initials, WSPU in the daily newspaper, regaling its readers with some of the wild acts that members of the group seemed to enjoy doing. Yet she had sensed from her readings of the articles that their cause was one she felt drawn to herself, if not necessarily to their methods. She hadn't realised that there might be a group so near at hand. Yes, she'd look forward to Annie getting in touch.

It was mid-afternoon when Annie sought her out. Rosie had had a busy morning and was sorting out the Political History shelf. It was heavy, dusty work. The books in need of repair had to be carried through to the small back office, where she spent time carefully examining them and making such repairs as she could.

It was as she came out of the office, weighed down with an armful of repaired books, that she noticed Annie's bright face smiling at her again from round one of the bookstands. With a conspiratorial jerk of her head, Annie indicated that she wanted to speak to her and they met at the end of the stand.

'I wondered where you were,' Annie

whispered. 'There's a meeting tomorrow night in the room over the Co-op in town. It should be good. There's to be a talk about the differences of approaches to the question of the enfranchisement of women by the NUWSS and the WSPU. We're expecting quite a crowd, so we need to be early. Do you want to come?'

'What is the NUWSS. Is it . . . '

'Another women's political union?' Annie interrupted. 'Yes, only the National Union of Women's Suffrage Societies is a mamby-pamby group. They hide behind our skirts and think that writing letters to members of parliament complaining of their lot is enough to get things changed. We believe in action! I tell you, things are moving. We've got to push on while the moment is ripe. So, what about it? Are you coming?'

Rosie pushed her vague disquiet about the more aggressive methods used by the WSPU to the back of her mind. Annie seemed too nice to get involved in anything too rowdy.

'Oh, yes, I'd love to! I've been reading a lot about it.'

She paused, thinking of her duties back home. Would they be able to manage for once? They wouldn't like it, she knew that, but unless she made a stand for independence, she'd sink into the mould they expected of her and her whole life would be wasted. She nodded eagerly.

'Yes, I'll come. Where shall I meet you?'

'We'd better meet outside the Co-op buildings, then we can go in together. Here, I've written the place down for you. I'll see you at seven o'clock. Is that all right? Don't be late.'

With a quick smile, she was gone, leaving an excited Rosie to continue her task.

'So, what do you think?' she asked Fred, later that evening.

She hadn't dared go without her brother's permission, even though it rankled deep within her that his permission was necessary.

'It sounds very interesting. I've been reading quite a bit about the movement and I agree with what they are aiming for. We women do have rights,' she added.

Fred looked up from the union notes he was reading. He was seated at the table with three open textbooks in front of him and numerous sheets of notes scattered over its surface. His brow was puckered in concentration.

'What was that?'

'I'll leave some stew cooking slowly in the fire-oven and I'm sure you can boil some potatoes between the two of you. Dad can keep an eye on it until you get home.'

Fred twisted round.

'Say that again. I wasn't really listening. A meeting, did you say? What sort of meeting?'

Rosie hesitated. The tone of Fred's voice put her on her guard. She could feel her night out slipping away from her.

'Oh, you know, something about helping us women to understand what the unions are about. It should be interesting.'

Fred grunted his disapproval.

'Union business is nothing to do with women. You'll never understand it.'

Rosie bristled.

'Is that so? Then you'll be pleased that we're making the effort to learn, won't you?'

'Huh! Some hopes of that! Anyway, who are you thinking of going with?'

'Annie Somers. She works at the library, in Ancient History.'

'Where's it at?'

'Over the Co-op buildings. It starts at seven so I won't be too late coming home.'

She deliberately didn't say it was the Bolton Co-op. If he chose to think it was local, it wasn't her fault, she excused herself a little guiltily.

'All right,' he said, 'but don't be late back. I'm not having my sister out on t'streets late at night. You'll be getting us all a bad name.'

Thus it was that, the following evening, after a hastily-eaten sandwich she had carried in her pocket, Rosie was walking quickly through the darkened streets of Bolton to the designated meeting place. Her heart was beating fast with excitement and anticipation. This was what she had longed for — a chance to use her brain and enter into the world where a woman could stand up and say what she felt.

Annie was already there, her head turning this way and that, looking out for her, white clouds of her breath escaping her mouth as she thumped her arms against herself to try to generate a little warmth. It was a cold evening. Annie's dark eyes lit up as she caught sight of Rosie. She grabbed her arm and pulled her through the doorway.

'Come on. We want to get a seat near the front. You can hear everything better from there. My cousin, Howard, is trying to save two seats for us.'

Rosie stumbled after Annie through

the chattering crowd. The large room was filled mostly with women, she noticed, though a few men were also in attendance. She was quite breathless when at last Annie pushed her into the second row from the front and they collapsed thankfully into the two vacant seats there. Annie leaned forward to speak around Rosie to the young man who was grinning delightedly at them both.

'Thanks, Howard. You're an angel. We'd have been stuck at the back, unable to hear a thing. This is Rosie Mather, by the way. Rosie, this is my cousin, Howard Baxter. He's a junior reporter on the Bolton Evening News. He has the brains of the family.'

'Annie has the scattered variety,' Howard quipped. 'How d'you do, Miss Mather? Are you another madcap, like she is?'

'I don't know. I'm not sure. Do you mean all this?'

She swept her hand around the babble about them.

‘Yes. Crazy, isn’t it?’

‘I suppose so, but it’s important, too. The more I hear about it, the more I agree with it. Why shouldn’t women have some say about what happens in the country, or even in their own lives? Surely the fact that women are now at some of the universities on equal terms with you men shows that they have equal brainpower! It’s high time that someone stood up and began to make an issue about it!’

‘You are as bad as Annie! Heaven help us!’

He rolled his eyes and dramatically slumped back in his seat. His comically derisive gesture went almost unnoticed as, at that moment, the noise in the hall hushed and then rose again as the enthusiastic audience applauded the arrival of the speaker and her entourage on the stage.

From the opening words, Rosie was riveted. Never before had she heard such fervour and impassioned rhetoric from any person, let alone a number of women, some hardly much older than herself. They debated the finer issues of tactics to further their cause, and from the use of words, it was clear that these were educated young women in the middle and upper classes. They weren't the brainless hoydens that newspaper reports tried to make out that they were. It was emotional and dramatic, but it was also a true portrayal of the unfair discrepancies that women suffered under in a male-dominated world.

So entranced was Rosie that she hardly realised what was happening when shouts were heard at the rear of the hall, followed by screams and sounds of scuffling. A distracted glance over her shoulder revealed nothing but when she looked back to the stage, the speakers had already left. The people around her were standing up and beginning to press their way along the row of fixed seats. Annie's alarmed face alerted her to the necessity of them moving also.

'What's happening?' Rosie asked in apprehension.

'Quick! Over here!'

Howard had leaped up on his seat and straddled his legs across the backs of the seats of the front row.

'Here! Give me your hand! Come on, Annie! You, too, Rosie! Quick!'

'What's happening?'

Rosie was bewildered. What on earth was going on?

'It's the police!' Howard hissed over his shoulder. 'They're here to break up the meeting and arrest anyone they can get their hands on.'

Rosie was puzzled. Why were the police here? Nothing untoward had been happening. She half turned to see what was happening behind them, but Howard pushed Annie in front of him and grabbed hold of Rosie's hand.

'Don't stop to look back! There isn't time!'

'But we shouldn't be running away like this!' she protested. 'We've done nothing wrong. It makes us look guilty.'

'Don't worry about that. Just run! Come on!'

Howard tried to pull her with him but Rosie couldn't grasp the urgency of his action and persisted in watching the mayhem at the back of the hall. She could see a number of hefty policemen wielding their truncheons and other men pulling and pushing at some of the women. That they were doing it none too gently was evident by the shouts and screams of their hapless victims. Rosie was incensed. How dare they?

Determined to intervene, she gathered the folds of her skirt into her hands and began to push her way to the back through those who were trying to escape by the exit at the side of the stage. The force of those trying to reach the front impeded her progress.

'Hey! You, miss!'

A burly man was climbing over the seats towards her, the belligerent expression on his face causing her to freeze in her steps. It was obvious that he meant her no good. She glanced back helplessly towards the centre of the uproar, now accepting that it would be impossible to help any of the women being attacked or evicted. The burly man's hand stretched out and grabbed hold of her arm.

'Looking for trouble, are you?' he snarled.

Rosie tried to jerk her arm away from his grip.

'All right, I'm going! Ouch! There's no need for that!'

Although the man was still in the row behind her, he was dragging her roughly along towards the side aisle, his fingers digging deeply into the soft flesh of her upper arm. The hem of her skirt caught on the edge of the seat support and she almost lost her balance. Her near fall dislodged the man's grip and she was now caught up in the flight of the last few stragglers rushing towards the side exit.

The force of their flight swept her along with them and she felt herself being unceremoniously pushed out into the street through the side door. The others continued their flight, the sound of their retreating steps ringing on the cobbled road and pavement. Rosie took some deep gulps of air, trying to regain her composure. Everything had taken place so swiftly she hadn't had time to take in what had happened. How had it started? What was the cause? And where were Annie and Howard? She looked up and down the street. There was no sign of them, nor anyone else now.

The evening mist and drizzle swirled around her. She could hear male voices shouting and laughing and realised they were coming in her direction. She looked around helplessly as a group of jeering youths emerged from the mist. No doubt they had been attracted to the scene by the general noise and, from the expression on their faces, had had some part in prolonging it. The tallest one laughed at her discomfort.

'What's up? Too lively in there, is it? Come 'ere! We'll take care o' thee!'

The youths formed a semi-circle around her. Rosie eyed them warily, backing away, but determined not to show how alarmed she felt.

'I can take care of myself, thank you very much!' she assured them, her pounding heart belying her brave words. 'You lads would do better helping us to fight for your rights in there than hanging about the back streets. Have you no wish to make something better of yourselves?'

'Hey, hark at 'er! Make somethin' of ourselves! What d'you fancy makin', eh, lads?' the tallest asked his companions. 'Ah know what I fancy!'

He made a gesture towards Rosie, drawing guffaws of appreciation from his companions. Rosie tried to back away farther but the lads now behind her pushed her forward again.

'Keep away from me!' she warned. 'Have you nothing better to do? I was in there fighting for the likes of you.'

'The likes of us, eh? An' what's a fine lady like you know about the likes of us?' one of the lads taunted.

'I'm not a fine lady. I was brought up not far from here.'

The previous taunter reached out and pulled her towards him.

'Fighting for me, was thee? Well, 'ere I am. You've got me. Tha's a bonnie lass. I'll show thee what's better to do. How about a quick kiss?'

The bristles of his unshaven chin scratched across her lips. She fought to retain her balance.

'Get your hands off me! Or else I'll . . . '

'Call a bobby? There's a number of 'em waitin' down the street for ye!'

He laughed as her free hand aimed a well-placed slap against his face. He grasped her flailing hand.

'A fire-brand, are ye? 'Ere y'are, lads! 'Ave a bit o' sport!'

He pushed her towards one of his mates, who spun her round and pushed her again towards another pair of outstretched hands. She felt a jerk at her sleeve. Her head was whirling and she was beginning to feel sick.

'Stop it! Stop it!' she screamed.

'Hey! You there!' a male voice shouted out of the mist, and the youths paused in their sport.

'Run for it, lads!' one commanded.

Rosie felt herself being swivelled round and round, then pushed one last time. As she staggered and tripped over the edge of the kerb, she heard the clatter of running feet and hoots of laughter as the boys fled.

She opened her eyes and found herself staring up into the concerned dark eyes of an extremely handsome young man.

3

Samuel Hardshaw had been strolling around the town centre of Bolton, familiarising himself with this, the largest nearby town to his new residence. His love of trains had brought him to work at the Locomotive Works in Horwich, a small town on the western side of Manchester and Bolton, but he now found himself missing the group of friends he had grown up with and with very few acquaintances made as yet.

Finding that Horwich night-life offered very little to interest a virile, energetic young man, he had made the eight-mile journey to Bolton on the local train, to weigh up what was on offer there. His steps had inadvertently brought him to Bridge Street, where the Co-operative building was situated. He hadn't known about the meeting that was being held there that night but the sounds of raucous shouts, women's screams and police whistles had caught his attention and he had followed the throng of other passersby who had joined the crowd of spectators.

'What's it all about?' he asked the man at his side.

'It's them women's lot . . . you know, them as throw bricks at people's windows and stick hat pins in bobbies!'

'Oh, suffragettes, they call themselves, don't they?'

'Suffrin' nuisances, more likely!'

Sam joined in the man's laughter and, hands thrust into his pockets for warmth, continued his way past the front of the building. He didn't take too much interest in the sight of some women of various ages being hustled into police wagons. No doubt they had broken the law and deserved any chastisement or penalty they received.

About to cross the road, he was suddenly aware of ribald laughter down the side street, partly obscured by the evening mist. The softer tones of a woman's voice reached his ears. The woman, whoever she was, sounded to be in distress, though she was bravely standing her ground.

Against his better judgement, Sam found himself being drawn down the street towards the jostling scene. He moved slowly at first, trying to discern exactly what was happening. He had no friends to back him up and he didn't want to be classified with the scuffling behind him. It wasn't his fight! A rough male voice sounded again. He heard the woman's desperate tones.

'Get your hands off me! Or else I'll . . . '

The man laughed and Sam heard the sound of what could only have been a slap against his face. He felt a surge of admiration for the young woman. She was a game lass, he'd give her that, even if she was one of these excitable, law-breaking young women he had read about. Through the thinning mist he saw the man take hold of the woman's raised hand.

As Sam began to move swiftly towards the scene, the ruffian pushed the woman at his mates, who spun her round and pushed her back again into other willing hands.

'Stop it! Stop it!'

The woman's cries were sounding desperate as Sam broke into a run.

'Hey! You there!' he shouted out, hoping to halt their unmanly sport.

He saw the youths, about half a dozen of them, hesitate and look in his direction. He knew he wouldn't have much chance against them if they decided to take him on, but he was counting on the element of surprise, and their evident moral cowardliness.

'Run for it, lads!' he heard one shout and, amidst a clattering of feet and hoots of laughter, the assailants fled.

Before he could reach out to grasp hold of the assaulted woman, she staggered and tripped over the edge of the kerb, falling into the road, where she lay winded for a moment or two. As he bent over to assist her, he could see that she was a pretty young woman, a girl, really, a year or two younger than he was.

'Are you all right, miss?' he asked, instantly berating himself for asking such a stupid question.

Of course she wasn't all right! She had just been manhandled by a gang of cowardly youths and was now lying in an undignified heap in the gutter. He could see a look of panic flooding her eyes.

'Leave me alone! Don't touch me!'

The girl struggled to get to her feet, pushing his extended hand away.

'You're all right, miss. I won't harm you.'

He held up his hands, palms towards the girl, backing away slightly as he spoke, though extending his hand once more as the girl struggled to rise. She pulled herself upright, refusing to take hold of his hand. He didn't blame her, not after the treatment she had just received. She made futile brushing movements with her hands on her clothes, finding a tear in her skirt.

'Drat!' she muttered to herself.

'It won't show,' Sam consoled her. 'You look all right.'

She did, too, he was pleased to note. Now that he could see her face more clearly he changed his mind about the word pretty he had thought about her. She was more than pretty. She was downright beautiful, even though her hat had come off and her mass of dark hair was tangled about her face. The girl sighed heavily.

'It will show when I arrive back home and I'll get what-for off my dad or my brother!'

She suddenly seemed aware that he was watching her anxiously and her eyes seemed to linger on his face and then swiftly assess the whole of him.

'Thank you for stopping. It was very kind of you.'

Her voice sounded tight and he suspected that she was fighting against the flow of tears that glistened in her eyes. He wanted to wrap his arms around her and hold her to him. He wanted to smooth down the tangles of her long hair and even drop a kiss on her forehead. He wanted to assure her that everything was all right, that he was here now and he'd look after her. But he knew he couldn't. She had had a nasty fright and any untoward overtures from him might unnerve her completely.

'I'm sorry I wasn't here sooner,' Sam apologised. 'Those louts deserve a good thrashing!'

'I expect I was more alarmed than I needed to be, but I admit I was frightened. I'm sorry I rebuffed your help at first. I didn't mean . . . '

Her voice tailed away as she fought back unwelcome tears.

'That's all right, miss. I could have been another of them for all you knew. My name's Sam Hardshaw. I'm a newcomer to these parts but I'm glad to have been of service to you.'

Heavens! Did he have to sound so

stilted! What was the matter with him?

The girl smiled.

'I'm Rosie Mather, and I'm glad you came along when you did.'

Her voice now sounded more natural and she thanked him once more.

'I'm all right now, honestly!'

She looked down at herself.

'My clothes! I'm afraid I must look quite a sight.'

She laughed self-consciously. Sam thought she looked wonderful but he bit back the words that would tell her so.

'May I escort you somewhere?' he asked, reluctant to let her go.

He couldn't quite equate this lovely young woman with what he had heard about the militant suffragettes. She sounded as though she had been well educated, though her voice held the local northern twang. She also seemed more level-headed than he would have expected a young woman of her leanings.

Rosie glanced up and down the street

once more, as though hoping to see someone.

'I was with some friends,' she said hesitantly, 'but they seem to have gone. I suppose I'd better make my way to the tram stop.'

'I'll come with you if you like,' he offered hopefully.

'Oh, I'm not sure.'

'I'll not harm you, miss, cut my throat and hope to die!'

He made the quick sign with his finger across his throat that had been part of the childhood ritual. Rosie laughed.

'I'll believe you, though I probably shouldn't.'

They walked to the end of the street, passing near to the main entrance of the Co-op Hall at the front of the building. Small clusters of people were still milling about but the major evictions seemed to be over and only one police wagon remained. Sam was aware that Rosie's footsteps increased in pace and he moved to the other side of her, placing himself between her and the policemen. She grinned up at him.

'I've never felt wanted by the police before. I'm not quite sure what happened in there but I think I must have broken the law somehow.'

'What did you do? Throw some fruit at the platform or something?'

'No!' she said, horrified at the idea. 'I wouldn't do anything like that.'

'You were probably just caught up in it all. I've heard that some women get up to some really wild things in the name of their cause.'

Rosie halted her steps and glared up at him.

'And what would you know? Have you been to any of the suffrage meetings?'

Sam grinned at her. She looked right wild with her hands on her hips like that. My, he wouldn't like to cross swords with her!

'No, I haven't,' he admitted, 'but I've read the newspapers. What do you hope to gain by all this militancy? Surely it must only lead to infuriating the authorities.'

Rosie dropped her glance and grimaced somewhat.

'I'm not really sure, as yet. It was my first meeting, but you must admit that women get a raw deal. We can't do any of the things you men can do.'

Sam took her words literally, taking her meaning to have been a simple regret for her female weakness. He felt a rush of protection for her.

'That's why you women need a good bloke to look after you.'

'I beg your pardon?'

Sam was surprised at the sudden coldness of her voice.

'Well, we men can do the things you can't, and you, well, you can do things we can't.'

'Such as? I suppose you mean cleaning floors and having babies.'

Sam groaned within himself. He was treading on dangerous ground here and realised he was in danger of putting his big foot in it. He didn't want to part company with this lovely girl on a wrong note. The town hall clock began to strike, ending his dilemma.

Rosie looked in the direction of the sound.

'Oh, no! What time is it? I'm going to miss the last tram. Oh, I must run! I'm sorry, Mr . . . er . . . Hardshaw. I must bid you good-night!'

Rosie offered her hand. Sam took hold of it but stood his ground.

'Sam, please,' he insisted. 'After rescuing you tonight, we must surely be on first-name terms, don't you agree?'

He tucked her hand over his arm and smiled down at her.

'I'll see you safely home, if you'll agree. I'll feel easier in my mind, after what's happened.'

'Oh, no! That's not necessary. As long as I get the last tram, I'll be all right. After all, I am a liberated woman.'

'Then I shall escort you to your tram stop. Er, which direction is it?'

'This way, but we must hurry.'

Rosie flung herself into a seat on the

tram and sighed a deep sigh of satisfaction. What a night! The final dash along Bridge Street and on to Deansgate had made talk impossible. The tram had been about to pull away from the stop and it was only because Sam hauled her along and almost flung her on to the platform of the tram that she had managed to get aboard.

She had stood on the platform looking back towards Sam's now distant figure, realising almost too late what his last words were.

'Where can I see you again?'

'I work at the library!'

Had he heard? Surely fate wouldn't be so unkind as to let her meet such a gorgeous man never to see him again. She recalled her first sight of him, towering over her as she lay crumpled in the road. He had the most stunning eyes! She felt her face go hot as she imagined the sight of her from Sam's point of view.

What had he thought of her? Her feminine instinct told her that he hadn't been too appalled by the sight of her, and he had bravely risked an uneven fight on her behalf, not like Howard who had made his own quick getaway. Just wait until she saw him again! She'd tell him what she thought of him and no mistake.

She pushed all thoughts of Howard to one side. Why think of him when she could think of Sam instead? A small smile played upon her lips. He was very good-looking. He was obviously of working class, like herself, but he spoke in better terms than most of the young men she knew from her schooldays. She was sure he had ambitions, maybe a bit like herself, though he seemed to have the typical working-class misconceptions of what women were capable of — or did all men think that way?

So deeply was she reminiscing that she almost missed her stop and it was only as the conductor pulled on the lever that jangled the signal to the driver to move on that she realised where she was.

'Oh, wait!'

She leaped up from her seat and sped to the platform, just managing to leap off as the tram began to move on its way farther into Horwich.

Fred was standing at the tram stop, his face furious with anger. His relief was evident when he saw her but his tongue was sharp.

'Where on earth have you been? I've been standing here for over an hour, and it's darned cold, I can tell you!'

'I didn't ask you to wait for me!' she said tartly. 'I can see myself home.'

'I'm not having my sister the talk of the street. Though what you mean by coming home this late, I don't know! What've you been up to?'

Rosie wondered whether or not to tell a few lies, but it wasn't in her nature.

'Er . . . the meeting was disrupted by the police. They seemed to think there was something illegal going on, but there wasn't. Honestly.'

'The police?' Fred stared aghast at

Rosie. 'Well, there must have been something going on. I thought you said you were going out with that Annie Somers you've met at t'library. Just what sort o' meeting was it?'

Rosie knew she looked guilty.

'I did say. It was . . . er . . . a sort of political meeting. Women's politics.'

'Women's politics!' Fred sounded both surprised and angry. 'I'd no idea that you were intending to go to one of those radical meetings. I'd never have let you go.'

Rosie flushed at his tone but lifted her head defiantly.

'What do you mean, you wouldn't have let me go? That's the very thing we are fighting for, the right to make our own decisions.'

Tight-lipped, Fred gripped her arm and set off quickly in the direction of their home, leaving his comments until they were in their own back kitchen with the door firmly closed against the great outdoors. Alf was there, sitting in his usual spot by the fire. He was soon brought up-to-date about the evening's events.

Rosie refused to be talked down to as if she were still a child. She placed the backs of her hands against her hips and stared at them defiantly.

'I can go where I want to!' she declared. 'I am interested in women's politics and I mean to find out more about it, so there.'

'Now, then, our Rosie. Fred 'as every right to be annoyed wi' yer!' her dad put in. 'Yer mam'd turn in 'er grave if she knew as yer'd got into trouble wi' police! We've never 'ad anyone from our family in trouble wi' t'law!'

Rose threw him an exasperated glance. She wasn't in trouble with the police! They hadn't caught her.

'Dad, I didn't do anything wrong. Nobody did.'

'That's what you say,' Fred broke in. 'These women deliberately provoke trouble and then they glory in all the publicity they get. They don't care who gets hurt.'

'It wasn't like that. Everything was going along fine until the police came charging in. They made all the bother. They were pulling people out of the hall and pushing them into the police wagons without giving anyone a chance to defend themselves.'

'So you say! What if it gets into the newspapers? Even local events like this hit the national papers if the editors can make a good enough story out of it. Just imagine what everyone round here would make of that.'

'So that's what's bothering you! Well, don't be ashamed on my account!'

Rosie's brown eyes were blazing like lanterns. She had expected sympathetic shock, not condemnation. She momentarily considered saying that Howard was a reporter and that they'd get a compassionate write-up, but thought better of it. The less she said about it, the better. Neither could she mention Sam's rescue of her. That would put the cat among the pigeons! Fred took her silence to mean that she was cooling.

'It's no use us quarrelling over it, Rosie. I'm sure you didn't know what you were going to. If Annie invites you to another meeting, you'll be able to tell 'er you're not goin'. If she's worth botherin' about, I'm sure she'll understand.'

Rosie gave an exasperated snort.

'Don't be so two-faced, Fred! You do all your union work. You know what it's like when you're up against authority. You've had fights on your hands. Well, so have we and I won't be waiting for invitations. I intend to get more involved in it all and help the cause as much as I can.'

Her face was flushed by her impassioned appeal. She was still in her outdoor clothes, her hat slightly askew, her hair wisping over her eyes. Impatiently, she pushed a stray lock behind her ears and then began to peel off her gloves, pulling at each finger with agitated movements.

'And don't think you can stop me, Fred!'

Fred's face darkened in anger. He gripped hold of her shoulders.

'I'm telling you it's not the right thing for young ladies to be doing. You'll not be going again.'

'I'll do as I want to. Tell him, Dad.'

Alf looked from one to the other.

'Fred's right, Rosie. It's for your own good.'

'But, Dad!'

She glared at the two men, unwilling to back down. At length, she sighed and looked away, knowing that it was pointless to pursue her argument right then.

'I'm going to bed. I've got a busy day ahead of me. Good-night.'

With that said, she stamped her way up the stairs. Men were going to have to learn that their domination over women was coming to an end!

4

'Rosie! What happened?' the hissed voice came, attracting Rosie's attention mid-morning of the day after the political meeting.

She was immersed in the repairing of some rather tattered books and glanced up swiftly. She shook her head at Annie, flicking her eyes to her left, indicating that Mr Vermont was within earshot. Annie nodded and swung her footsteps in Mr Vermont's direction.

'Here you are, Mr Vermont, some more books for repair. Shall I give them to Miss Mather?'

Mr Vermont frowned at her.

'A little less noise, Miss Somers, if you please. Miss Mather is in the next aisle. You may take the books to her quietly, but please do not linger. We are extremely busy in this department.'

'Yes, Mr Vermont.'

She smiled charmingly at him before turning on her heels and tripping lightly to the far end of the aisle.

'What happened to you last night? We were 'way down the next street before we realised you weren't with us! When we went back, you'd gone!' Annie whispered.

Rosie hastily cast her eyes about.

'I can't talk here. Meet me at lunch time.'

An hour later, Rosie recounted the events of the previous evening. Annie seemed to be slightly disappointed by what she was telling her.

'Oh, we thought you must have been arrested,' Annie pouted. 'I was full of envy, I can tell you. Why don't you let Howard know what happened? It could be good publicity for us. You know, unprovoked attack and all that.'

Rosie was aghast.

'It was very frightening, Annie. I was terrified about what the youths might do to me, and I certainly don't want to be plastered across the front page of the local paper. My dad and Fred would be livid.'

'We have to make the most of every opportunity, Rosie. Anyway,' she added, leaning forward, her eyes shining brightly, 'there's another meeting at Farnworth next Tuesday evening. Are you coming? We'll be more prepared this time.'

Rosie shook her head.

'I'd better not, Annie, not so soon after last night. Fred really was very angry. I think I'd better keep a low profile for a while.'

'You'd better watch out, Rosie. I wouldn't let my brother or any other man order me about like that! Anyway, I'll let you know how we get on.'

Rosie thought over their conversation when she was back at work, a little disturbed by Annie's willingness to flout authority so readily. What good had her experience last night done for the suffrage cause? Very little, it seemed, except get her into trouble with Fred.

'Miss Mather, may I have a word, please?'

Rosie sighed. Just what she didn't want was trouble with Mr Vermont. She looked over to where her colleague, Geoffrey Brown, was surreptitiously reading a newspaper folded inside one of the order books. He seemed to escape all condemnation. With a sinking heart she saw that Mr Vermont was clutching an early edition of the local paper in his hand. He placed it heavily on the table in front of her. She read the headline: **Local Woman Arrested In Riots at WSPU Meeting**.

'Am I to surmise that the Miss M who works in one of our libraries in Bolton refers to none other than yourself, Miss Mather?' Mr Vermont asked with eyebrows raised in incredulity.

Rosie met his gaze and trembled under its intensity.

'I was at a meeting,' she agreed reluctantly, 'but I wasn't arrested.'

Mr Vermont thrust the newspaper

into her hands, the relevant paragraph circled in red. She could feel her cheeks burning as her eyes swiftly scanned over the offending article.

Police officers called to the event . . . infiltrated by militant activists . . . near riots . . . missiles thrown on to the stage . . . many arrests made . . . Miss M who works in one of our libraries in Bolton arrested.

She gasped in dismay. How could Howard? It was nothing like it had really been! Her eyes blazed with anger.

'I was there, Mr Vermont, but I assure you that it was nothing like this article portrays.'

She hadn't been aware that she had risen to her feet until she had finished speaking and found herself meeting Mr Vermont eye to eye.

'Come to my office, Miss Mather, if you please.'

Mr Vermont paced to his office. By the time Rosie arrived he was already seated at his desk. For the next five minutes he subjected her to a severe lecture on the proprieties of public behaviour by municipal employees and how it was their duty to remain above reproach on all occasions. Rosie stood with hands clasped in front of her, marvelling to herself that she managed to remain silent throughout the tirade. She sensed that her job depended upon her meek acceptance of his stern lecture.

'What have you to say for yourself, Miss Mather?' he asked finally.

Rosie controlled her voice. She decided to start with an apology.

'I'm sorry, Mr Vermont, but, as I said earlier, I was at the meeting, but I assure you that I did nothing to warrant arrest. And neither did most of the other unfortunate victims of what I can only call police harassment.'

She took a deep breath and, since Mr Vermont was still looking at her in silent appraisal, she continued.

'It was an orderly meeting until the police arrived and I was enjoying listening to the speakers. I didn't agree with everything that was said, but I found the various views interesting and was shocked by the disruption.'

Mr Vermont leaned forwards, the tips of his fingers meeting.

'Miss Mather, I find myself in a dilemma. If one of my young men had appeared in such an article, I would have no hesitation in dismissing him instantly. However, I feel compelled to put the episode down to your naïvety and misplaced fervour and have no wish to appear prejudiced against your fairer sex.'

Rosie felt hope stir within her.

'Thank you, Mr Vermont.'

'However,' he repeated firmly, 'I want your assurance that you will not put yourself again into a position that might lead to any repetition of such an article about any of the employees in this library. Do you understand?'

'Yes, Mr Vermont.'

She wanted to say more, to protest that she hadn't invited the attention of the Press, and that neither would she promise to give up her pursuit of the suffrage cause, but she left it all unsaid, preferring to accept the olive branch being offered to her.

As she returned to her table, she was uncomfortably aware of the conflict that warred within her. Annie, she was sure, would have told Mr Vermont exactly what to do with her job. Had she, herself, somehow let down the women's cause by her reticence?

Back at her desk, she worked hard for the rest of the day. She half-hoped that Sam might somehow come to find her, but he didn't. She consoled herself with the thought that he was probably working.

A triumphant Fred greeted her on her arrival back home.

'I've managed to let one of our rooms to a paying lodger,' he told her. 'That'll mean more money coming in, and you'll be able to give up your job once the first few weeks have been paid for.'

'A lodger?' Rosie echoed. 'What room have we got for a lodger? And what about cooking his food? Who's going to do that?'

'You are, of course!' Fred answered. 'You'll 'ave plenty of time once you've given up your job. And, as for the room, I've already moved into the front room. The lodger can have my old room. It's all settled, isn't it, Dad?'

'But, Dad!'

Alf knocked out his pipe against the stone mantelpiece.

'Aye, it is, lass. I never thought to see the day we'd 'ave to start takin' in lodgers, but there you go. Times is 'ard and we 'ave to do what we can.'

Rosie scowled. It was bad enough having two men to look after. Now, there'd be three! And she didn't need to be a genius to know whose back the extra work would fall upon.

'He's coming round to see 'is room after tea,' Fred informed her next, 'so make sure everywhere's looking nice.'

Rosie glanced around the room. There wasn't much in it to make the room untidy. She removed her coat and hung it by its loop by the door and then looked at the stew that was simmering over the fire. It looked ready to be eaten. She tested the potatoes that Mrs Blackstock had put on to boil. They, too, were ready.

The meal was eaten in near silence. Rosie was brooding over Fred's new demand that she give up her job. It wasn't fair. She had settled down nicely and she knew Mr Vermont was quietly pleased with her work. She was standing later at the stone sink washing the dishes when a knock sounded at their front door.

'That'll be 'im,' Fred asserted, rising from his chair. 'Now, make yoursel' pleasant to 'im, our Rosie. We need the brass he'll be fetchin' in.'

Fred opened the door. Rosie had turned back to the sink. She wasn't going to fall over herself making the lodger welcome. It was the sound of his voice that froze her hands among the soapsuds and made her turn slowly. She couldn't believe her eyes. It was Sam!

She felt a hot blush rise up her cheeks. How had he managed it?

Fred's voice was making the introductions and Rosie suddenly feared that Sam might inadvertently give away the fact that they had already met each other. That wouldn't do. Fred would be livid. Sam, however, was merely smiling pleasantly in her direction.

'Miss Mather,' he murmured in greeting.

He then winked audaciously across at her, causing her to blush more furiously in her confusion.

'Er ... how do you do, Mr Hardshaw?' she stammered, wishing that her hands and arms weren't covered in soapy bubbles. 'We've just finished tea and I'm washing up,' she babbled.

'So I see.'

He smiled. Aye, Rosie was a great-looking lass!

'You keep the house nice and cheerful, Miss Mather,' he complimented her, grinning broadly when she lowered her eyes.

He turned towards Alf and strode across the room towards him, his hand outstretched.

'Good evening, Mr Mather. I'm right pleased you've agreed to take me. I'll be no bother to you, I assure you.'

His eyes had already taken in the general tidiness of the room. His first glance around had shown him that the mid-terraced house, though sparsely furnished, was neat and spotlessly clean, even though the area lay in the shadow of mills and factories that spewed out filthy clouds of smoke all day.

He had expected no less. Fred had already told him that their mother had died a few months earlier and that, since his dad's accident at the foundry that had left him crippled for life, his sister had, until recently, been the full-time housekeeper for her father and brother. He had hardly dared to believe that Fred's sister was Rosie when he had read the hand-written notice on the works' notice board. The surname was the same, but there might be any number of Mathers in the town.

He could have kicked himself last night when he had suddenly realised that he didn't know where Rosie lived and had made no arrangements to see her again. What must she think? She probably thought he didn't want to see her again! In the same instant that he had realised that the tram was heading for his own destination and knew he could have boarded it with her, he had desperately called out his question. He had barely heard her reply and thought he must have misheard it when his visit to the Horwich library that afternoon had proved fruitless. The woman behind the desk hadn't heard of a Rose Mather, and that was that.

He had hastily returned to the Locomotive Works and found Fred Mather just as he was leaving for home. The proposed accommodation sounded ideal and he had made the arrangement to view it that evening. Seeing Rosie's face, and instantly deducing that she hadn't mentioned their meeting the previous evening, he was glad that he hadn't asked Fred the question that was burning in his heart. Though not a deceitful person by nature, he reckoned it was best to keep quiet about it, for Rosie's sake as much as his own.

'I'll take ye upstairs, lad,' Fred was now offering.

Sam left Rosie's presence reluctantly and followed her brother upstairs. He was pleasantly surprised by the size of the room being offered to him. He realised that Rosie's share of the other divided area was smaller than this and hoped she didn't mind.

Rosie had watched the two men leave the room and mount the wooden staircase to the upper floor with mixed feelings. She felt weak at her knees at his unexpected appearance and confident handling of the situation but she felt full of dread in case he still betrayed their previous meeting. Fred would think they had connived the present course of action and would probably throw Sam out of the house. She put the kettle on the hob and brewed a pot of tea for when they came down.

When the two men once more entered the kitchen both their faces were wreathed in smiles. Fred invited Sam to sit down at the table to discuss terms with him and Rosie poured strong tea into two mugs.

'Milk and sugar, Mr Hardshaw?' she asked.

'Yes, please, and call me Sam, won't you?'

His smile melted her insides.

'And I'm Rosie,' she said artlessly.

She knew better than to join them. She pulled her chair over to the other side of the fireplace from where her dad was sitting and smiled at him. She could read the sense of shame he felt at the need of taking in a lodger and she reached out to touch his hand.

'It'll be all right, Dad,' she said silently.

'Aye,' Alf agreed sadly, drawing on his pipe.

Rosie let her gaze wander to where Sam and Fred were sitting. Sam's profile was towards her and she unashamedly studied him. He was a well-made man. His body was all muscle, broad shoulders, no doubt built up from his work as a boiler maker. He was dark haired, brown-eyed, and had lovely, even teeth that gleamed white, revealing that he didn't smoke like most lads she knew. She would be proud to be seen out with him.

She was pleased to overhear that he spent three evenings each week at the Local Mechanics' Institute and he requested use of the table to do some studying on the other evenings. Fred agreed. He approved of a man who hoped to better himself. When Sam got up to leave, Rosie rose with him.

'I'll see him out, shall I, Fred?' she offered brightly.

They didn't speak other than to wish

each other farewell, but their eyes spoke volumes.

'I'll bring my things over tomorrow, after work,' Sam promised as he took his leave.

'We'll be delighted to make you feel at home.'

Rosie smiled, thankful that Fred couldn't see the delight on her face, in case he might have second thoughts about having Sam as a lodger.

Rosie then made up the bed in what would be Sam's room with clean sheets before retiring for the night, in case she didn't have time in the morning. Life was looking promising, she decided as she smoothed down the top cover.

She flung herself into her work over the next two days, aiming to win approval of her dedication to the job. She loved every minute of it. As soon as the library closed for the night, she sped happily along to the tram stop, eager to be home to see Sam. She discovered that he was easy to talk to and didn't mind conversing with her dad. The better he got on with her brother and father, the more pleased she was. On the second evening, Sam helped Fred to assist Alf to make it to the local pub, his first visit since his accident, and it was worth the couple of hours on her own, darning socks, to see the renewed light in her dad's eyes on their return.

Wondering if they could ever have some time on their own, Rosie was suddenly aware that Sam was speaking to Alf about the very subject.

'Would it be possible for Rosie and me to walk out together on Sunday afternoon, Mr Mather?' she heard him say.

Rosie held her breath, knowing she would be unable to bear it if her dad refused. She needn't have worried. Slowly, he nodded his head.

'Aye, if the lass is willing, and if you are willing to bide by certain conventions.'

'Of course. I mean to court Rosie properly and won't do anything to harm her reputation,' Sam replied quietly.

Rosie felt as though her heart would beat its way out of her chest as both sets of eyes turned towards her.

'Oh, yes, please,' she agreed, hoping she didn't sound over eager or unseemly. 'I'll look forward to that!'

It was two whole days away! How would she last until then?

5

The hours at work sped by and Rosie would rush from one source of delight to the other, to cooking tea for Sam and an evening spent talking and sharing their thoughts, all closely supervised by Alf or Fred.

Sam intended to study and rise through the grades of his chosen profession. He had ambitions and made Rosie aware that he would expect to be able to support a wife without her needing to go out to work. Rosie disagreed. Her yearnings were for a sense of independence and, to her, a job was part of the means of attaining that independence.

She shared her new-found objectives within the suffrage movement with him, her face alight with the thrill of it all, brushing aside Sam's doubts as to the validity of her endeavours and her enthusiasm. He would understand if he knew more about the movement, she assured him, scorning Fred's interventions of his views of women's suffrage. Women's unions were as valid as men's unions, she argued heatedly.

In the predominately male household, her views were discounted, ridiculed, even though Sam kept the love light shining in his eyes when he told her so. The look in his eyes took her breath away, halting her fervent assertions. She longed to be alone with him.

Sunday dawned at last.

Rosie awoke early, long before it was light enough to get up. She lay still for a while, thinking how strange it was that Sam was lying in the next room. She wondered if he, too, was awake and was he as eager for their planned walk as she was?

With Sam's extra money she had been able to buy a pound of bacon and half a dozen eggs and she took pleasure in cooking a fried breakfast for them all, though she felt unable to eat much of it herself as her stomach felt full of butterflies. Sam didn't seem to have any trouble in clearing his plate. His praise for her cooking made a happy glow spread through her and she wondered briefly if she were more cut out for a life of domesticity than she had thought. Cooking for Sam and hearing his praise beat cooking for her dad and brother at any rate, she decided.

She rushed through preparing the vegetables for Sunday lunch whilst the men read their Sunday newspapers, reflecting that the unequal sharing of household tasks used to infuriate her. But it was grand now having a small joint of brisket to cook, milk and eggs for the Yorkshire pudding and plenty of vegetables. She had even put a milky rice pudding in the lower oven to cook slowly whilst they were at church.

Walking to church in front of Fred and Edie, her hand linked through Sam's arm, Rosie basked in the envious glances she received from several unattached girls.

After church, as soon as their dinner was over and the dishes washed, dried and put away, she rushed upstairs to brush through her hair and don her coat again. Sam had scrubbed his skin until it shone and looked resplendent in his jacket, high-collared shirt and trousers. Then, to Rosie's chagrin, it became evident that Fred and Edie were to accompany them.

'That's not fair!' she protested. 'No-one goes out with you and Edie!'

'Are you planning to do something you would be ashamed to be seen by Edie and me?' Fred asked coolly.

'No, of course not!'

'Then what's your problem?'

'Fred and I are a bit older than you, Rosie,' Edie put in. 'We can be trusted not to misbehave.'

Rose's eyes narrowed and she said, 'Meaning?'

'Well, if the cap fits, you wear it,' Edie suggested unwisely.

'How dare you?'

Rosie was furious. She didn't dare look at Sam. She felt so humiliated and was sure he must be despising her.

'Come on, Rosie,' Sam's steady voice invited her.

He took hold of her hand and laid it on his arm, patting in possessively. He bent his head down and whispered in her ear.

'Take no notice. We've all the time in the world to be alone together.'

Placated, Rosie did as he asked and they set off up the street. They took the tram so far, then headed for a hillside which was a popular destination for the local people on such a beautiful day. Mingling with other couples, overtaking most of them, Rosie soon forgot their other company and enjoyed the walk. By this time, Sam had taken her hand in his and the touch of his skin sent tingles through Rosie. Sam frequently bent to whisper words of endearment, making her cheeks blush.

As they reached the lower slopes, Sam cast a glance over his shoulder.

Fred and Edie had dropped behind a little, unable to keep up with the younger couple. He eyed the square watch-tower on the summit.

'Race you to the top!' he challenged Rosie.

Her eyes shone.

'Catch me if you can!'

Letting go of his hand and picking up the front of her skirt, she whirled away, squealing with feigned fright as he charged after her, caught up with her and passed her.

'Wait for me!' she called.

Sam halted until she drew level. He then took hold of her hand and set off again, pulling her with him. It was exhilarating and exhausting. When they reached the top, she sank down against him. Fred and Edie were far behind, still struggling up the lower slopes.

Sam drew Rosie round to the other side of the tower, away from the others. The initials carved into the stones of the tower bore witness to other couples who had visited the spot. Sam leaned against the stone tower and drew Rosie close to him. Rosie's head felt as if it were spinning out of control. She closed her eyes as he held her. Sam tilted her face up towards him. She could feel the warmth of his breath as he spoke.

'I wouldn't kiss you quite as quickly as this,' he apologised, 'only I think we'll have to make the most of the time we've got!'

With that, he lowered his face towards her and gently placed his lips on hers. It was Rosie's first real kiss and she felt in seventh heaven. Time stood still. The kiss could have lasted for eternity. It was Sam who drew apart again, holding her slightly away from him.

'Rosie Mather, you are lovely. Are we . . . you know, walking out together?'

Rosie grinned mischievously, spreading out her hands.

'It certainly looks like it!'

Sam caught hold of her hand and pulled her close.

'Will you be my girl?' he whispered.

'Yes.'

Sam took hold of her hands and stepped away from the tower, swinging Rosie round, their bodies leaning outwards away from each other. Rosie looked upwards. The few puffy white clouds, pristine against the bright blue sky, seemed to spin round and round them.

At length, Sam slowed down their twirling. Out of the corner of his eye, he had seen Fred and Edie arriving at the summit, neither of them looking too pleased. Sam casually draped his arm around Rosie's shoulders and pointed westward to where he could see a glint of the sea.

'What's over there?' he asked.

Rosie followed his glance.

'That's Southport, and farther north is Blackpool Tower. Can you see it?'

She pointed to the far horizon. The air was so clear on this fresh spring day that the metal structure was faintly visible.

'I'll take you there in the summer,' Sam promised.

Monday brought them down to earth. A stolen kiss in the kitchen sent Rosie to work with a glow on her face and a sparkle in her eyes. The world was beautiful, and everyone in it.

She wondered if Howard would visit the library to apologise for his inaccurate newspaper reporting of the events at the meeting, but he didn't, and Annie didn't pop in to see her either, nor the next day, before the meeting in Farnworth that Annie planned to attend, nor during the morning afterwards. As soon as lunchtime arrived Rosie slipped upstairs to her department and quickly searched for her friend.

'May I help you?' a middle-aged man asked her.

Rosie took him to be Mr Dodds.

'I was hoping to see Miss Somers for a moment. Has she gone to have her lunch, do you know?'

Mr Dodds shook his head.

'I'm afraid that Miss Somers hasn't come into work this morning, neither has she let me know why. I am supposing that she must be unwell.'

'Oh! I'm sorry to hear that. Thank you.'

Rosie made her departure. She didn't know where Annie lived, so there was no way she could discover the reason for her absence. As she ate her sandwich, she realised that one possibility would be to go to the Bolton Evening News offices and ask to see Howard Baxter. He would know where Annie lived and might know whether or not Annie was ill. Rosie couldn't help feeling slightly apprehensive about her, with good cause, as it turned out.

She had been back at work for only ten minutes when she saw Howard slipping into the library and making his way towards her via a number of bookshelves that he made show of perusing. At last he stood before her.

'Have you heard about Annie?' he asked quietly.

Rosie looked up sharply, instantly apprehensive.

'No! Why? What's happened?'

'She went to the meeting last night as planned and, when one of the opposing speakers wouldn't answer her question about his support, or lack of it, for the enfranchisement of women, she began to throw eggs and fruit at him!'

Howard grinned.

'It isn't funny, Howard!' Rosie protested in dismay. 'I'm not sure that throwing things at people is a very good advertisement for our cause. What impression does it give of us?'

'It shows you mean business,' Howard replied. 'But that's not what I've come to tell you.'

He leaned forward, his voice taking on a conspiratorial air.

'She was arrested and taken to prison. I tried to get her out but she wouldn't have it. Preferred to get locked up and make her protest more strongly. She's game, I'll give her that. I should get a good story out of it.'

'Like you did from me?' Rosie demanded, her voice louder than she intended. 'Your report was nothing like what happened. How could you?'

Howard grinned sheepishly.

'It was a bit wild, wasn't it? Not my fault, though. Another of our reporters was there as well. He's senior to me and my article was incorporated into his. It made a good story, though, didn't it?'

'Not in my opinion! What's the point of writing things that aren't true?'

'Jackson wrote it as he saw it. He was farther back and saw some women with baskets of rotting fruit, which they began to hurl after we left the hall.'

She felt so upset by Howard's attitude.

'Miss Mather! How many times must I tell you that this library is not a public meeting place? Kindly tell your friends not to intrude upon your working hours.'

Rosie jumped as Mr Vermont's voice hissed in her ear. Thoroughly startled, she swung round to face him, sending her inkpot flying across she table to land upside down on the parquet floor.

'Oh! I'm sorry!'

Her hands flew to cover her horrified face.

'Oh! Quick! The blotting paper! Where is it?'

She searched for something to mop up the pool of ink that lay accusingly across her work. How the flying inkpot had missed the pile of books that she was to work through next, she didn't stop to marvel at. Mr Vermont looked furious.

'Move the books!' he snapped. 'And the papers! Not those! The clean ones!'

He snatched the books out of her hands and hugged them to his chest, more alarmed at what might have happened than the actual event.

'Hey! It wasn't Rosie's fault!' she heard Howard remonstrate. 'Don't blame her for it.'

'I shall blame whom I wish, young man. And I suggest that you make yourself scarce before I call for help to have you evicted forthwith.'

'Please go, Howard,' Rosie insisted. 'Your presence isn't helping.'

Acceding defeat, Howard went. Rosie hastened to clear the area, her hand shaking with agitation. However had it happened? One minute she was entering the details of a book into the ledger, and now, just look at the mess!

Her usual commonsense returning, she dived into the small back room and emerged with a cloth in her hand, which soaked up the ink on the desk more efficiently than the blotting paper. Most of the ink, she now realised, was on the surface of the order forms that she had completed earlier in the afternoon, though a dark stain ran from there, over the edge of the desk and on to the floor, where it joined the small pool around the upturned ink pot.

She hastily dropped down upon the offending pool with her cloth. Her brain raced over remedies she had seen her mam use for ink stains. She glanced over the polished, wooden floor. It bore a variety of stains, albeit less vivid than this latest. Water would have to do for now. At least that would dilute the stain. She looked at her hands, her ink-stained fingers. Thank goodness Mr Vermont insisted on her wearing a dark skirt. Any marks there wouldn't show.

As her jumbled thoughts calmed down, she stood up slowly.

'I'm sorry, Mr Vermont. I'll get some water.'

She looked at the order forms.

'I'll stay late and re-do the orders.'

'Get out!' he hissed. 'Just leave. Go after your friend. I knew it wouldn't work! Incompetent females!'

Rosie looked at him in dismay.

'I'm sorry, but it wasn't entirely my fault. You did creep up on me and make me jump.'

'I don't want to hear any excuses! Just go! Any wages due to you will be sent to your home.'

Rosie stared aghast at him. Maybe she had misheard? But she hadn't.

'You're fired, Miss Mather,' Mr

Vermont hissed, leaving her now in no doubt as to his intentions, 'as from this moment.'

With another almost incomprehensible look at him, she turned and fled. She just wanted to get away from his anger and the curious stares of the silent readers in the library. Her heels tapped smartly against the wooden floor, until she reached the strip of carpet that ran down the main aisle. The contrasting quietness soothed the edges of her shame and she managed to shut the swinging doors noiselessly behind her.

Grabbing hold of her coat from the cloakroom, she rushed from the building and ran down the steps, her eyes now nearly blinded by unshed tears. She almost collided with a darkly-clad figure.

'Sorry! Oh, it's you!'

It was Howard. His anxious face looked down on her.

'Rosie, what's happened? I was coming back to try to take some responsibility. Why have you left? Are you all right? You seem upset.'

'Upset? Can you blame me? Oh, Howard, I've lost my job.'

Howard searched his pocket and produced a large, cotton handkerchief.

'Here, use this.'

He put his arm around her shoulders unsure how best to comfort her.

'There, now. Is that better? Look, let's walk towards the river behind the church. What happened after I left? Was it my fault?'

'Yes, it was! Did you have to come in there to tell me about Annie? You know what Mr Vermont is like.'

'I'm sorry. I thought you'd want to know.'

'I did, but . . .'

Her throat tightened and no further words could be said. Together, they walked up towards the parish church that stood at the top of the hill. Howard kept his arm around her, aware that her body was still shaking.

Rosie didn't object. There was

nothing to object to. He was a friend, giving comfort, and she had been unfair to him, really. He might have sparked off the incident but she was already in Mr Vermont's bad books, simply because she was a female. He had only been awaiting such an excuse to fire her legitimately.

Neither of them saw Sam come out of Prestons', the jewellers' shop on the corner. He had gone there, the largest jewellers in the north of England, with the thought in mind, that, if he knew the cost of an engagement ring, one that would be worthy of his love for Rosie, he would know how much money he had to save before he could formally ask her to marry him.

The sooner the better, he couldn't help thinking, then she would focus her attention on preparing her bottom drawer. Left to himself, he'd marry her tomorrow, no matter how empty the drawer might be!

Mulling over the cost of the various rings he had looked at, Sam glanced casually along the street, then stopped and stared, as the oblivious couple walked on their way. Rosie! And her companion was a man! He had bent his head down to speak something close to Rosie's ear. She lifted her face towards him, obviously replying, though Sam couldn't hear the words.

The man laughed and pulled Rosie closer and, in seeming harmony, they sauntered on up the hill.

6

Sam's face went red, then white. The initial shock turned to anger, but he didn't know what to do. He hoped that there was a reasonable explanation for what he had seen, but he couldn't think of one!

Back at the house, Sam tried to get on with some studying but the image of Rosie with another man, walking arm-in-arm, kept forcing itself into his mind. Why wasn't she at work? What had happened, and who was the man? The questions tormented him. He now wished he had rushed up to confront them, but he hadn't wanted to face what might have been an unpleasant truth, not in a public place.

He dropped his head into his hands, glad that Fred had taken Alf to the public house on the corner. Where had he gone wrong? Why had Rosie turned to someone else? He loved her so much. Wasn't his love for her enough? He couldn't bear it! Oh, Rosie, where are you? Come home!

The sound of the door latch lifting made him leap up from his chair and he was at the door before it was fully opened. As he grasped the doorknob and pulled the door towards him, Rosie almost fell at his feet. She staggered towards him, and his outstretched arm caught hold of her.

'Oh, Sam, you're home! I've been so . . .'

The faint scent of cigarette smoke on her hair wafted past his nostrils. Rosie didn't smoke. Neither of them did. The smell inflamed his couple of hours of worry into waves of anger. He pushed her away from him.

'Where have you been?' he demanded angrily, looking at her far from neat appearance. 'And just look at you! Straight from a tousle with your lover, are you? Well, you look a disgrace.'

Rosie staggered back as if she'd been

hit. Her face whitened.

'What do you mean?'

His face twisted with derision. He just wanted to hurt her, as he had been hurting for the last two hours. His bitter words tumbled out.

'Don't think you can just walk back in here as though nothing has happened. You must have taken me for a blind fool. Been canoodling with him up some back alley, have you?'

Her eyes stared in blank amazement at him. She couldn't believe what she had heard, not from Sam! She crouched back against the door, her hands covering her ears.

'No, I haven't, Sam! I haven't!'

Sam was immediately appalled at the effect that his words had upon her. He had wanted his words to hurt her, but now he wanted to take them back. He hadn't meant them. He knew they weren't true, didn't he?

'Rosie, I'm sorry. I didn't mean it. Forgive me! Please, forgive me.'

He tried to take her in his arms but

now she pushed him away.

'Don't touch me! Don't you dare touch me!'

A furious anger began to blaze within her. She straightened up to her full height. What she lacked in inches, she more than made up for with her spirit. She faced Sam squarely, her conscience clear.

'I saw you,' he said, 'walking up towards the church with a man, draped all over you, he was. And you weren't exactly fighting him off. Is that what you've been up to at these so-called meetings of yours? Ah, I see I've hit the mark, haven't I?'

If it weren't so serious, Rosie's expression might have been thought comical. Her first reaction of relief that it was nothing serious brought the glimmer of a smile to her face, but it was quickly replaced by another blaze of anger. He was accusing her of being unfaithful to him. How dare he!

'I met Howard at my first meeting, yes. Meeting, note, not meetings! I have been to one meeting only.'

'You didn't mention him.'

'Why should I? I didn't even know you then.'

Once she had met Sam, her encounter with Howard had faded into insignificance. She wasn't going to tell him that, however, not in the face of his present attitude. She glared at him defiantly before continuing.

'He is Annie's cousin and he is also my friend. He was consoling me.'

'Consoling you! What for? Having to put up with a simpleton like me who is easily duped? Is that what he thinks? Of course! You haven't told him that you are walking out with me, have you? You must think I'm an idiot.'

'No, I'm the idiot.'

For loving you, she almost added, but bit back the words.

They glared at each other. Then, the spirit seemed to ooze out of her. She dropped her gaze and turned away from him. Where was the loving man who had held her in his arms and kissed her tenderly? She was used to Fred ranting and raving at her when he was displeased, but this was different. Sam loved her, didn't he?

She suddenly felt very close to tears and spoke quietly.

'You're cold and distrustful. I suddenly don't know you any more.'

'Cold? I'll show you how cold I am!'

He pulled her to him, one hand in the small of her back, holding her against his body. His other hand held the back of her head, as his mouth searched for hers.

'Don't, Sam, not like . . . '

Her words were cut off, as her lips were enclosed in his. With a passionate intensity he didn't know he had, his mouth embraced hers. When she felt his mouth lift from hers, she stood still and leaned against him, wondering how their anger had turned to passion so quickly. Sam's rage had taken her completely by surprise. She had never seen him so angry before, but if seeing her with someone else had made him so angry, it must mean he loved her a lot. He wasn't to know how innocent it all had been. With a contented sigh, she nestled her head into his chest.

Sam's anger had faded and the intensity of his love shone. As Rosie saw the tension had faded and the gentle love he showered upon her had taken its place, she, too, relaxed. She reached up and touched his face gently.

'I was upset, Sam. I've lost my job. I spilled ink all over my table and the floor. Mr Vermont shouted at me and told me to leave.'

Sam stroked her hair.

'I'm sorry, love. I know how much your job meant to you.'

'Do you think I should go back to him and apologise? I bet I could get rid of most of the stain.'

Sam kissed her brow, then her eyes, then her cheeks.

'Why not stay at home now? You've got my money coming in and I know Fred isn't happy about you working in the library.'

Rosie shook her head.

'I'm not giving in that easily. I think I could persuade Mr Vermont to take me back.'

'You'd be more certain of getting your job back if you'd give up all this talk about women getting the vote,' Sam urged her. 'I know you are intelligent and I suppose your friend, Annie, is as well, but you've got to admit that most women we know wouldn't have a clue whom to vote for.'

Sam seemed oblivious to Rosie's stiffened body and continued blithely.

'I mean to say, take Fred's young lady, Edie. She's a bit vague when it comes to political issues. All she wants from life is to be married and have a whole host of babbies clutching her skirts.'

'And whose fault is that?' Rosie demanded.

'I wouldn't say it was anyone's fault. It's just the nature of most women. It's a known fact that most women's brains aren't as large as men's brains.'

'I beg your pardon!'

Rose stepped away from him, her face livid with anger.

'I suppose some weak-kneed, lily-livered man wrote that statement, did he? I'd like to see the size of his brain, I would. I bet it would fit in a thimble!'

'Eh, come on, now, Rosie. Don't go and be getting stroppy at me again. I thought we'd settled all that.'

'You might have settled it to your way of thinking, Sam Hardshaw, but you haven't settled it to mine. What you men don't seem to realise is that we aren't only fighting for votes for women. There are still thousands of men who haven't got the vote. What have you got to say about the size of their brains, eh? In fact, Sam Hardshaw, it isn't all that long ago since men like you have had the right to vote, so think yourself lucky that someone was brave enough to stand up and fight for it.'

'That's different. We men understand what it's all about. Most women would have to ask their husbands whom to vote for anyway, so they may as well just leave it to them in the first place.'

Rosie stood, hands on hips, waiting for him to finish.

'And is that your last word on the subject, oh, great and mighty one?'

'Since you ask, yes, it is.'

'Well, this is my last word. I'm going to get my job back, and I'm going to continue fighting for the vote. Oh, and if you want your tea, it's in the pot in the fire-oven. I'm going to visit Cissie Jenkins.'

And on that slightly childish note, she strode to the door.

'Don't bother to save me any. Suddenly, I'm not very hungry!'

* * *

Dressed with her greatest care, Rosie left home early the following morning and returned hopefully to the library. Mr Vermont listened politely to her apology for what had happened and her intention of cleaning up what she could of the ink stains on the floor and table. However, at the end of her halting words, he shook his head.

'I am sorry, Miss Mather. Your work was impressive, beyond my expectations, but my misapprehensions about employing females in my department were fully justified. I am not prepared to take the risk again, especially with a female as young as you are. Your friends and followers pose too many problems!' His expression softened a little as he added, 'Come back in twenty or thirty years' time. Maybe you will be acting in a more sober manner by then.'

Rosie's hopes sank. She murmured a quiet goodbye, and left the building. What was she to do with herself? She wasn't prepared to slink back home and take up the rôle of housekeeper again. She needed a worthwhile job. She wondered if there might be some suitable positions in the local paper, but was too ashamed to return to the library to look through the advertisements. A sudden thought brightened her. There were other libraries with copies of the daily newspapers for the public to read freely, her local library in Horwich, for one.

With no more ado, she caught the tram back to Horwich and made her way to the library. A pleasant-faced young woman was on duty. Rosie smiled tentatively at her. There was often a more elderly man in charge, but he was nowhere to be seen. It was good to see a woman in charge.

She found where the newspapers were kept but her eager eyes dulled somewhat when she could find nothing in the least bit suitable on offer. She banged a clenched fist on to the table in an outward show of her disappointment.

'Is everything all right?' a quiet voice asked behind her.

Rosie turned round to find the duty librarian regarding her in concern. Rosie grimaced apologetically.

'I'm Sorry. I shouldn't let my frustration show like that. I've just lost my job at the library in Bolton and I thought I'd look to see what was on offer around here.'

'A librarian, eh?' the woman asked. 'What position did you hold?'

'Only a junior position, I'm afraid, very junior,' she added ruefully.

'Why did you leave? Were you sacked?'

Rosie felt her face flame as she nodded.

'I hadn't really done anything wrong. It was mainly because Mr Vermont there doesn't really think women are capable of the job. I don't know why he gave me the job in the first place. I was the only woman at the interview. He could have chosen one of the others, if he had so wished.'

'There have been some moves amongst the hierarchy to give us weak females a trial, in subservient positions only. I'm just the assistant here.'

She hesitated, carefully weighing up

Rosie's demeanour and personality.

'The fact is, I really need to go part-time for a while. My mother is ill and I don't like to leave her all day on her own. I've been paying someone to go in and see to her whilst I'm at work but my mother can be quite sharp at times and Mrs Calder says she's not willing to continue. I've been at my wits' end, I can tell you!'

Rosie leaned forward eagerly.

'And do you think I might be accepted? Oh, if only I could.'

'I don't see why not! By the way, my name's Charlotte Thornhill. What's yours?'

'Rosie Mather.'

'Right, Rosie, I'll give you a form to fill in and you can leave the rest to me for the time being. I'll speak to Mr Perkins when he comes in this afternoon but I'm sure he will agree to give you an interview. He already knows of my problem and will be pleased to have so speedy a solution of it. Come back tomorrow morning and I'll tell you what he says. Oh, would you be able to do mornings, by the way? It takes me ages to get Mum up and dressed, so afternoons will suit me much better.'

'Yes, that's fine. I'm in a similar position to you, except it's my dad who's the invalid. My brother sees to getting him up in the morning so there's no difficulty there. In fact, they'll more than likely be pleased that I'll be home to give them their tea, instead of leaving them to dole it out themselves.'

Charlotte laughed.

'And they try to make out we're the helpless ones!'

She looked thoughtfully at Rosie.

'Are you interested in the women's movements at all?'

'I am indeed! That was partly the trouble. I attended the meeting over the Co-op in Bolton last week and got caught up in some of the violence afterwards. I'd done nothing wrong, except be there!'

She went on to explain the events,

ending with the spilled ink and her subsequent dismissal.

'So now you know the whole story,' she concluded. 'Do you think I'll be deemed suitable for the position here?'

'Eminently so, by me. I was only asking because we have an active NUWSS branch here in Horwich. We don't go in for the same witless actions of our more militant sisters. Why don't you come along to our meeting next Thursday?'

Rosie beamed.

'Wonderful! Since I am going to be working part-time, maybe I could do some work for the branch in my spare time.'

'Indeed you may. I've a feeling we're going to get on fine together, Rosie. Look, I'll write down the address of our president, Mrs Leatherbarrow who lives along Scholes Bank. Do you know where that is?'

'Yes, just past the Crown Hotel, isn't it?'

'That's right. You could pop along

there this afternoon. She'll be more than pleased to see you.'

And, indeed, the lady was. By the time Rosie was on her way home, she had committed herself to four afternoons a week helping in a makeshift office in Mrs Leatherbarrow's front room!

7

After what could only be described as a perfunctory interview on the Friday afternoon, Rosie agreed to begin her new job the following Monday morning. Sam was pleased that she had got herself a new job so quickly but was less sure about her commitments to the women's group.

'I thought we had agreed that you were going to give up all that nonsense.'

'You might have agreed but I didn't. Besides, this group isn't as militant. They believe in more peaceful means of achieving our aim and, I must admit, I'm inclined to agree with them. I really can't see how throwing eggs at someone gets support. But that doesn't mean I'm going to stop going to meetings and rallies,' she added quickly. 'I'll probably stay on in Horwich after helping at the centre on days we have our meetings, as it won't be worth coming home. I'll leave your tea cooking.'

Fred wasn't happy about it either. He scowled at her.

'Your place is here in this house, Rosie. You know nowt about politics and never will. I won't be letting Edie go off to these meetings. She'll do as she's told.'

'Well, I'm not Edie,' Rosie retorted, 'and you're not Sam.'

'No, he's too soft wi' you. You want to toughen up, lad!'

Sam eyed him firmly.

'I'll keep her in check in my own way,' he stated calmly.

Rosie glared at the two of them.

'I'll set my own limits, if it's all the same to you.'

Her heart beat rapidly. Sam must be made to see that it was her duty to throw herself wholeheartedly into the movement, and if he didn't, then they must agree to disagree. Whichever, she wasn't going to turn back. She lifted her chin high and faced them.

'It's no wonder we women have wakened up to demand our rights. We're sick and tired of being told to keep our place and stay tied to the kitchen sink. What right have either of you to tell me what to do with my life?'

'We have the right because we give you our protection,' Fred informed her shortly. 'A lass on her own wouldn't last long.'

'So you say! From whom do I need to be protected?'

'Yourself, by the sound of it,' Sam said, trying to make light of it. 'So, calm down and let the subject drop for now, whilst you're on top.'

Rosie grinned at him.

'Do you mean you have no objections?'

'I have some, but I'm willing to let you go your own way for now,' Sam acceded. 'But don't push me too far. I won't be made a fool of.'

No, Rosie agreed, he wouldn't, but then, that wasn't her aim, so everything would be all right.

She and Sam walked out together on Sunday afternoon, their set-to forgotten by Sam, and pushed to the back of her mind by Rosie. Their destination was nearby Lever Park, a developed area of land given to the people of Horwich and Bolton by Lord Lever. New roads, lined by trees, meandered between paddocks housing deer, buffaloes, zebras, emus, yaks and other animals never seen before by first-time visitors.

Sam and Rosie strolled hand-in-hand, weaving in and out among the other Sunday afternoon strollers, trying to evade the over-watchful eye of Fred and Edie, who dogged their footsteps yet again.

In a wooded area on the shore of the reservoir, Rosie once more tasted the delights of a secret kiss. So what if Fred knew what they had been up to whilst briefly out of his sight! They ended their hours of freedom in the Saxon Barn, a renovated structure where refreshments were available. Sorry as Rosie was for the day to end, she was also filled with a mixture of excitement and apprehension about the start of her new job next day.

Mr Perkins, her new senior, was more approachable than Mr Vermont. He had equally good standards of work and high expectations of his juniors, but his mellow side was more discernible and, although his library was a quiet place of work, Rosie realised quickly that she didn't have to walk around on tip-toes or be afraid to smile once in a while.

Charlotte had agreed to come in on Monday morning to help to settle Rosie into the job. Because of her time spent at the library in Bolton, it wasn't as strange as it might have been and Rosie felt well-able to dispense with Charlotte's assistance on Tuesday.

Everything went smoothly at the library on Tuesday morning and Rosie made a point of staying until Charlotte arrived for the afternoon session before leaving. She brought her up-to-date with her morning's work and had the pleasure of hearing Mr Perkins speak favourably about her to Charlotte. A bit of praise went a long way, she reflected.

Mrs Leatherbarrow greeted her warmly when she arrived there afterwards.

'Come right in, dear. It's a pile of letters this afternoon. Can you type?'

Rosie's face fell.

'Not very well, Mrs Leatherbarrow,' she admitted. 'I've been using the typewriter at the library, but I only use two fingers, I'm afraid.'

'Call me Mildred, dear. Everyone else does. And not to worry about the typing. You'll soon pick it up. Here's some paper. Give me a shout if you need help. I'm just through there. We've got a Bring and Buy on Thursday and I'm baking some biscuits to sell.'

As the afternoon progressed, other young women came and went. Some stayed to work on some various projects, others brought posters done at home or called to collect instructions on what to do next. Rosie had to drag herself away and catch the tram home. Life had never been so exciting.

On Thursday lunchtime, as she prepared to leave the library, Mr Perkins beckoned her to his side.

'Yes, Mr Perkins?'

'I just want to congratulate you on your efficient manner of working and your swift acceptance of the tasks you had been shown, Miss Mather. Now, make sure you enjoy yourself at the meeting tonight but don't get too excited and volunteer to fill every vacancy.'

His eyes were twinkling with good humour and Rosie was glad that he didn't mind his two junior librarians working for women's suffrage.

'Mrs Perkins is an active member,' he explained to her. 'She's on one of the regional committees, so I'm sure you'll see her.'

Rosie did see her. Mrs Perkins was organising the northern committee that had been set up to co-ordinate their campaigning locally and nationally.

'We have to know what each group is doing, ladies,' she announced. 'We must work together and be seen to work together. Focus on full suffrage for all, ladies, and, one day, we'll achieve it.'

Her words heartened everyone and when another of the ladies, a Mrs Cook, asked for volunteers to do some door-to-door canvassing in the district, Rosie found herself rising to the call. Sam usually practised running with the Railway Mechanics' Institute athletic team on Saturday afternoons, so Rosie offered to distribute her share then.

When she was rushing home on Friday, knowing she was just in time to see to dishing out the casserole of shin beef and vegetables that she had left cooking all day, she was both surprised and pleased to see Annie waiting for her at the top of their street.

'Annie! You're back! How are you?'

Rosie was glad Annie hadn't been kept in prison for too long, but Annie's face looked pinched, in spite of her bright smile, Rosie thought. The two girls hugged each other. Annie's eyes were shining brightly.

'You know I've been in prison, don't you?' she asked Rosie.

'Yes, Howard told me. What happened? Was it like at the meeting I was with you?'

'Yes, but a lot worse! This time we were more prepared. We fought back when they tried to drag us out into the street. Just wait until you see the bruises on my arms!'

Rosie was unsure how far she approved of Annie's actions.

'What was it like in prison? Was it quite dreadful?'

Annie grimaced.

'It was no picnic, I can tell you. They didn't actually ill-treat us but it's a pretty Spartan existence, and a humiliating one. You have no privacy, for anything. Warders can be watching you at all hours of the day.'

'But didn't anyone complain? It must have been awful for you!'

'Oh, we complained, all right. Not that it did us much good. Anyway, when our complaints weren't listened to, we decided we would go on hunger strike. They released us all after four days, when we were beginning to get weak, so it wasn't too bad. My mother says I look a sight, though. She didn't want me to go back to work but I was determined. You could have knocked me down with a feather when Howard came round and told me you'd been sacked, so I wasn't too surprised when the same happened to me as well.'

Rosie was shocked to hear what Annie had been made to endure.

'I don't know how you could bear it, Annie. Weren't you frightened?'

'A bit, especially at night, but it's over for now, until the next time!'

'You won't get arrested again, will you?' Rosie asked incredulously.

'I might,' Annie said flippantly. 'They tend to let us protesters go and then arrest us again when we've put a bit of weight back on. Anyway, Howard said he's missed you. He tried to get your address off Mr Vermont, but he wouldn't give it to him. I think he fancies you. Shall I tell him where you live?'

Rosie was aghast at the idea.

'Oh, no, that wouldn't do! I'm walking out with Sam. He'd be very upset if Howard visited me.'

'So, what are you doing now? Have you got a new job?'

Rosie brought her up to date on her work front and enthusiastically described her new voluntary position with the women's group. Annie wasn't impressed.

'We'll never get anywhere if we wait for politicians to simply give us the vote. We have to fight with any means we can get our hands on, if that means throwing a brick at someone, then I'll do it!'

Rosie was dismayed. She truly didn't think it was the right way to go, and she hated losing her friendship with Annie, but she also couldn't condone the extreme actions she had both heard and read about. Annie refused to go home with Rosie for a cup of tea. Her face showed her condemnation of Rosie's more passive views.

'I'll see you around, then, Rosie.'

Rosie watched sadly as Annie turned and crossed the road to catch the tram back to Bolton. She knew she had lost a friend.

March came in with blustering winds. The woodlands were aglow with daffodils and crocuses and buds swelled on the branches of the trees, filling the air with promise.

Rosie's weekday activities now kept her extremely busy. Lunchtimes were spent at Mildred Leatherbarrow's home, where she penned letters, designed and painted posters and pamphlets and addressed countless envelopes. Her keenness was noted, as was her ability to hold her own in the lively debates that frequently broke out there.

At a meeting in April, after delivering a lively report on the combined efforts of all the willing volunteers, Rosie was approached by Mrs Perkins with the suggestion that she might care to join the team of ladies who went up on the platforms of horse-drawn wagons positioned outside factory gates in the dinner hour and spoke to the crowds of men and women who gathered to hear what they had to say.

Rosie felt her heart race.

'Do you think I could?' she asked breathlessly. 'I've never done anything like that before.'

'Neither had any of us before our first attempt,' Maud Perkins assured her. 'You'll be good at it, I'm sure. You have a good way with words. You're young, and pretty enough to attract attention. Weather permitting, we've got a few venues booked next week. Will you give it a go?'

Rosie nodded.

'I'm sure I'll be scared to death, but, nothing ventured, nothing gained, as my mam used to say. What shall I talk about?'

'Talking is hardly the right word. Shouting is more like it! We won't put you on first, so you'll be able to get the feel of it.'

They were to speak outside Victoria Mill first. Rosie didn't dare tell Sam about it. She knew he wouldn't like it and she didn't want to provoke an unnecessary quarrel with him. He was a good man and she loved him. When they weren't arguing about her rôle in the women's movement, they were in harmony together on everything else. She knew life would be empty without him. She just wished that he could understand what she was fighting for.

When she arrived at Mrs Leatherbarrow's house to meet with the rest of that day's team, she was dismayed to discover that the venue had been changed. They were now going to speak outside the gates of the Locomotive Works, where Sam worked!

She was tempted to excuse herself, but when two of the other women had had to send in their apologies due to their children being unwell, Rosie felt compelled to stand by her commitment. More than likely, Sam wouldn't attend the meeting. He had heard all their aims and aspirations from her and wouldn't want to hear it all over again.

A large, horse-drawn wagon had been hired and drawn up outside the works' gates. A set of wooden steps was placed at the back of the wagon and the ladies trooped up the steps and set themselves ready to face the crowd. Rosie had no idea what to expect. She felt she would have been curious to hear what this set of people had to say and would have pushed to the front to be able to see and hear better, maybe even be prepared to ask questions. But she was totally unprepared for the stampede of feet and jostling bodies, not to mention the whistles and catcalls. How on earth were they going to be heard?

As she mounted the wagon, she scanned the gathering crowd. Sam would stand at least half a head taller than most of the men and he clearly wasn't there. Maud Perkins had volunteered to start, and Rosie was surprised to see her take a large clock from her bag and hold it aloft. She began to speak quietly. Even Rosie, who was standing only a couple of feet away couldn't hear what she was saying and she felt like shouting to her to speak up, but to her amazement, the crowd gradually quietened themselves and Maud simply repeated what she had been saying before, now in more strident tones.

'Time is ticking on, ladies and gentlemen. We have been campaigning for the enfranchisement of all adults for over forty years and have got nowhere. How long are they going to keep us waiting? When are we going to be given a say in what happens in our country?'

From then on, Rosie hardly heard a word, she was so nervous. When Maud turned round and nodded to her, she swallowed hard. Her moment had come! She had been primed to talk about children's rights, and, sending up a fervent, silent prayer she stepped forward.

'What about your children?' she began. 'Who looks after their rights?'

'We do!' a man shouted. 'I look after my kids, all right!'

'And do you decide that they have to leave school at twelve years old and work as many hours as you do for a few pennies a week?' Rosie challenged him.

The man looked abashed, but answered, 'Well, it's the law!'

'And who made the law? I'll tell you. It was men with no thought of how tired the children become.'

Rosie lost her fear and her words, held so passionately within her heart, flowed out into the crowd. There were hecklers, but she took their jibes in her stride. She had been brought up amongst them. She knew how they thought and how they felt. She was aware of some cheers echoing around the fringe, possibly from some of their regular supporters who often encouraged them by being present and keeping the meeting warm by their spontaneous reactions. But the sound of the cheers faded as the focus of her attention was grabbed by the figure of a man pushing his way through the crowd, a look of sheer anger on his face.

It was Sam!

8

Rosie was frozen into immobility. It felt like a nightmare where she was trying to run away from something but her feet wouldn't move. The scene passed as if in slow motion.

Sam was forcing his way through the crowd, pushing people aside as he strode forward, his eyes fixed on her face, and then he had leaped up on to the wagon and had grabbed her arm, furious.

'You're coming home with me!' he almost snarled at her and Rosie had never seen him so angry, his face as red as she was sure hers was.

A few men cheered and catcalled but Rosie barely heard them. The whole focus of her attention was on Sam and his public humiliation of her.

'Let go of my arm!' she said, dangerously quiet.

Sam hadn't really intended to attend the well-advertised meeting. He had left the casting shop with his mates and had unthinkingly walked towards the gates. It had been the familiar tones of Rosie's voice that made him look up and, from then on, he had been drawn forward as if by a magnetic force.

He had barely broken his stride as he leaped up on to the wagon and his only thought was to remove Rosie from the centre of that group of stupid, foolish women whose husbands, if they had any, ought to have been there beside him, exerting their authority over them. He was aware of Rosie's resistance of his action but he was beyond caring. When she refused to follow him towards the steps at the rear of the platform of the wagon, he did the only thing he felt was possible.

He grasped Rosie around the waist, and lifted her headfirst over his shoulder as if she were as light as a petal of blossom. With her fists flailing at his back, his hands carefully holding her skirt wrapped around her furiously kicking legs, he side-stepped nimbly down the set of steps and strode through the now-cheering crowd of men. A pathway opened for them as if by command and Sam looked neither to the left nor the right.

He didn't pause until they were well clear of the crowd.

'Put me down, Sam Hardshaw!' Rosie yelled furiously, still pounding his back with her fists. 'Put me down at once! Do you hear?'

'I'll put you down when you stop screaming and kicking!' Sam shouted back, his temper still high, fuelled by the evident glee of the young lads.

He'd been made to look a fool and was in no mood to act with caution.

'You can put me down immediately, and the moment you do, I am going straight back to the meeting and getting back up on that wagon and continuing from where I left off when you so rudely interrupted me.'

To her surprise, Sam lowered her feet

to the ground but he immediately grabbed hold of her wrists in a vice-like grip.

'Oh, no, you're not!'

His fiery face was less than an inch from Rosie's, and if she hadn't been in high temper herself, his expression would have made her heart quail within her. As it was, it merely fanned the flames of her passion. She tossed back her head and met his glare eye-to-eye.

'And who are you to forbid me?'

'Your husband-to-be, that's who, and if you think you can carry on with this unbecoming behaviour, then you need to stand back and take stock of yourself and seriously consider our relationship.'

Rosie glared at him, her eyes flashing dangerously.

'That's a fine thing! You say my unbecoming and wilful behaviour yet, you are the one who has roughly manhandled me in front of all those people. How could you?'

She struggled to free her hands, with the intention of once more pummelling his chest but Sam's grip was too tight.

'Let me go, you brute!'

'Not until you calm down and promise to go home quietly.'

'Never!' she spat out.

'Then it seems I must take you there!'

'Don't you dare touch me again. I swear I shall bring an action of assault against you. You are not my husband yet, and, after today, I vow you never shall be.'

She hadn't planned to say that. It just came out of her mouth without time for thought. For only a split second did she regret the words. Then the memory of her humiliation hardened her resolve and brought a sudden calmness to her demeanour.

'I mean it, Sam. We're through!'

The colour drained from her face and her eyes hardened.

'I think I almost hate you right now. I want nothing more to do with you.'

It was the change in her voice, the now calm fury, that made Sam realise that she meant what she was saying. He stared at her, the cold finality of her voice cooling his anger with an icy dowsing. He didn't regret his action. He knew he would react in the same way again, even if he had had time to think through what might become of it, but he was shocked, all the same.

They glared at each other for what seemed an age, neither face betraying the turbulent thoughts that were cascading around inside each head. It was Sam who broke the silence.

'Then that's that,' he said coldly. 'You've made your choice. I will find myself some new lodgings and move my belongings out of your father's house as soon as I can. Maybe you had better go home and tell your father that I am no longer his lodger. He may wish to advertise for someone else. I have to go back to work.'

He paused for a moment, wondering if she would say she hadn't meant it and implore him to reconsider, but she didn't. They stared blankly at each other, both trying to take in the finality of their stance, neither wanting to be the one to back down. Sam turned away first. Rosie watched him as he strode back towards the works. He'd be late. It could cost him his job. Serve him jolly well right!

Her heart felt strangely cold and empty, more empty than it had been before she had known him. Her body missed his touch already. If he had stopped and turned to look over his shoulder, she would have swallowed her pride and run after him. She almost did so anyway, but the memory of his words held her in its grip and her feet remained where they were.

The group of boys was still there, quiet now, as if sensing the heartbreak within her. She knew there was no point in returning to the meeting, even if it hadn't been in the same direction as Sam was going. She hadn't heard the works' hooter but she knew it must have sounded. The other ladies would have packed up and gone, and she couldn't face them now anyway. She couldn't face anyone.

She turned and began to walk in the direction of her home, her step heavy. She heard the rumble of a tram coming along the lines behind her, but she didn't want to catch it. Tears were streaming down her cheeks and she needed time to compose herself. Sam was going. He was finding new lodgings. Commonsense told her that he had no alternative. They couldn't live in the same house after this, but the family would miss his money, and Fred was talking of getting married to Edie Fisher soon. How would Rosie and her dad manage then?

Her hands clenched at her sides and her lips set in a determined line. They would manage! She would make sure of that, somehow.

It was Monday before Sam actually moved his belongings into his new digs. He didn't say where he had spent the intervening nights and Rosie didn't ask. Her dad and Fred had directed their anger at her, with no apparent thought of protecting her honour. They did not mince their words when they told her angrily how stupid they thought she was over the whole women's movement business. No matter how she stood up for herself and voiced her rights, they both condemned her angrily for her actions. She had never seen her father as angry as he was the night Sam moved out.

'I order thee to get up them stairs!' her dad said sharply once Sam had gone. 'Tha's been disgracing the family with all yer shenanigans. Count yersel lucky I can't get up an' belt thee one!'

He'd never been a violent man and Rosie knew she had been more gently reared than many of the other girls in the street. However, she knew now, from the tone of his voice, that he meant what he said.

'I'll go,' she said quietly, 'out of respect for you, Dad, but don't think you can browbeat me into changing my mind, because you won't.'

She had the presence of mind to fill a beaker with water and she stalked upstairs with her head held high. Although it was early, and she had had no tea, she wasn't hungry. She had a raging headache, partly from the crying she had done and the tears that were still bottled inside of her. She loved Sam, had loved him, she made herself think. She was sure that she would never love another man as she had loved him. The memory of his smile, the tone of his voice, even his frowns and anger, were now bittersweet.

Oh, Sam, come back, she moaned inwardly, but she knew he wouldn't. She would have to beg his forgiveness and promise never to take part in her suffrage activities again. However much her heart was crying out for his return, she knew that she could never turn her back on the campaign for women's right to vote.

Even so, life without Sam now seemed very bleak indeed and she wished that the day's events hadn't gone the way they had.

The days that followed seemed long and dreary. Rosie found herself looking for Sam's familiar figure as she travelled home on the tram all that week, or waited at the tram stop. Each man who entered the library sent a flutter through her body, followed by a deep sense of disappointment when it wasn't Sam.

She told Charlotte what had happened. Her friend was sympathetic but would allow her no self-recriminations.

'Men are either for us or against us, and the majority are against. Not many change their minds, I've found. You'd best forget him, and count yourself well-rid!'

Rosie nodded miserably.

'Yes, I suppose so. I'm dreading the meeting on Thursday. What did people say after last time?'

'It provoked some lively debate. Mildred Leatherbarrow made the most of it, I can tell you. Typical male bombastic behaviour, she called it. A man thinking through his muscles instead of his brain!'

She grinned at Rosie.

'Nobody is going to forget that meeting in a hurry. You'll be famous, hailed as a heroine, I should think.'

Charlotte's prediction wasn't far off the mark.

Howard walked into the library one day towards the end of the week.

'Why wasn't I at that meeting?' he bewailed. 'I could have got you front page status. Let me know next time you intend to pull a stunt like that.'

'It wasn't a stunt, Howard. It was for real!'

'I didn't think you would go in for cavemen tactics. Sam must have you just where he wants you.'

'Sam hasn't got me at all. We've split up, and there's no need to look so pleased about it.'

'Sorry,' Howard apologised, still smiling.

'You don't look very sorry.'

'No? Well, it's good news for other

admirers, isn't it?'

'Is it?' Rosie said, unimpressed. 'I'm not looking for other admirers. I've decided to dedicate myself to the cause from now on.'

'That's all right. I'm dedicated to it as well. We can be dedicated together, can't we? I like dedicated suffragettes.'

'I'm not a suffragette. I'm a suffragist. There's a subtle difference.'

'As long as the road leads to victory, I don't mind which one you actually tread. Actually, someone as level-headed as you could do your cause a great deal of good publicity. I asked Annie to write up something about her experience in prison but my editor decided it was too dramatic. He said no-one would believe the half of it.'

'And who is he to make that judgement?' Rosie demanded. 'Annie told me what it was like and it all sounded perfectly believable to me.'

'Yes, but you don't know Annie as much as I do. When we were kids, a scraped knee became a broken leg in her telling. What we need is someone like you to write a dispassionate account, all the truth without all the frills!'

Rosie looked at him swiftly.

'I hope you're not suggesting I get myself arrested, merely to determine the truth of the matter.'

'Well, no, but if it happened, it would be a pity to waste an opportunity like that, wouldn't it?'

Rosie thought no more about it. Whatever their more militant comrades might aspire to, she had no intention of getting arrested. Howard suddenly smiled.

'Anyway, I'm not here to talk about votes for women right now. I came to see if you would like to accompany me to the Theatre Royal on Saturday night. I've been asked to do a review and have a spare ticket. It's a shame to let it go to waste. Would you like to come with me?'

'You have a rare way of tempting a girl!'

‘What you see is what you get with me, but, if it makes you feel any better, I immediately thought about you when I was given the tickets.’

‘I’ll believe you. Yes, all right, I’d love to come.’

It wasn’t a good idea, however, as Rosie was miserable the whole evening. She couldn’t help it. It was as if her love of life had dissolved, leaving her empty. Howard tried to make her smile, but the faint glimmer he managed to raise from her was a poor substitute.

After two days of absolute misery, Rosie decided she would have to swallow her pride and find where Sam was now living. She was too proud to ask Fred and had to resort to waiting opposite the works’ gates, hoping to catch sight of Sam as he left work. When he emerged, he was in the midst of a group of other workmen.

Rosie’s breath caught in her throat at the sight of him. She longed to be able to reach out and touch him, to be held in his arms, hear his whispered endearments. Her longing was so great that she had actually raised her hand to hail him when a female voice called his name.

'Sam! Sam Hardshaw!'

Rosie saw his head turn, his eyes searching for the source of the call. She saw the look of recognition flow over his face and followed the direction of his glance. Betty Draper, a girl who used to be in the same class as Rosie at school, was waving eagerly to him and beckoning him. As Sam bade his workmates farewell and moved in Betty's direction, Rosie felt her heart lurch. It hadn't taken him long to replace her, had it?

At that moment, something made Sam turn his head and for a brief second, their eyes met. Sam made a move towards her but Rosie saw Betty pull on his arm, saying words Rosie couldn't hear. Rosie made herself give a scornful toss of her head and turn away, ignoring Sam's call of her name. She was taken aback by how hurt she felt deep inside. Her face set like granite, she strode away quickly in the opposite direction.

If he was satisfied with Betty, he deserved his fate, Rosie consoled herself. No doubt he had found his submissive woman. Well, let him be bored to death. She didn't care. But she knew she was fooling herself. She did care. She cared very much indeed.

9

Charlotte Thornhill reminded Rosie that a member of parliament was speaking at a meeting in Farnworth on Wednesday evening.

'Are you still coming, Rosie?'

Rosie felt little enthusiasm for the meeting.

'I'm not sure. I think I'll give it a miss this time.'

'You've got to snap out of it, Rosie. You mustn't let a man, or the lack of one, ruin your life. Come on. It'll do you good. It's Ewan Barnsley, you know, the one Mildred Leatherbarrow was saying always sits on the fence until he sees which way to fall. We might be able to give him a timely push.'

In spite of her lethargy, Rosie was stirred by her friend's pleas.

'Go on, then, since you insist. I'll come.'

'Oh, good! I knew you would.'

She delved into her bag and drew out a slim envelope.

'Maud Perkins asked me to give you this.'

'What is it?'

Rosie turned the envelope over and read her name on the front.

'It's a question to ask Mr Barnsley after his speech. The question has been cleared by his campaign team.'

'What's the catch?' Rosie asked suspiciously.

Charlotte laughed.

'You're sharp, I'll give you that. When he has answered the question, before you sit down, you ask another question. In this case, ask him outright whether or not he supports the campaign for total suffrage.'

'He won't like that.'

'That's the idea! Will you do it?'

Rosie felt a stirring of her passion for suffrage. Maybe it was just what she needed to get her out of the doldrums. She nodded.

'Yes. I'll do it!'

The meeting couldn't have gone better. Ewan Barnsley gave a middle-of-the-road speech and sat down to a smattering of applause. Questions were invited from the floor and various men and women rose in turn to ask their submitted question. Mr Barnsley made his replies, attracting applause from the right-hand side of the hall. Rosie suspected he had planted supporters seated there. It was a frequently-used ploy.

At last, it was Rosie's turn. Her heart was thumping as she rose to her feet to ask her initial question. It was a low-key question about child welfare proposals. The timing of her next question was crucial. She got it spot on.

'Will you support the fight to give every adult the right to vote?'

For what seemed to her to be an eternity there was silence as the speaker's face changed colour a number of times. Then, within the space of seconds, a number of people, men and women scattered around the hall, jumped to their feet, cheering and clapping loudly. Immediately, others stood to voice their objections. Shouts and whistles rang through the air and, to Rosie's horror, fruit, eggs and other missiles were being thrown at the men on the platform. Scuffles broke out, and voices were raised as each side vied with the other.

A louder uproar erupted near the rear of the hall. Screams pierced the shouting and a full-scale brawl seemed to be breaking out.

'I thought known troublemakers were being screened out by us having entry by ticket only. Who's started this?' Rosie gasped to her neighbour.

Chairs were being tossed around. Men and women were grappling with each other, arms flailing and legs kicking. It seemed as though everyone was throwing in their lot. People were being pulled out of their seats into the narrow aisles. Others were attacked where they sat. Rosie and others rushed towards the fighting, pulling at those nearest to them.

'Stop it!' Rosie yelled. 'Which ever side you support, this doesn't help!'

Police whistles sounded and the surging crowd began to fall back, knocking over those who were too lightweight to stand firm. Rosie found herself trapped between two rows of seats, now in the midst of the fighting. Helmeted police officers were forcing their way through the tumult, truncheons flailing. Rosie felt a sharp stab in her arm.

She whirled round to see a wild-faced young woman about to stab her again with a long hatpin. She grasped hold of her wrist, deflecting the aim.

'Hoyden!' the woman screamed at her, attempting to stab Rosie again and again. 'Yer nowt but a trollop, a disgrace to womanhood.'

Rosie felt her face blanche at the unfair accusations. She used her free hand to wrest the hatpin out of the woman's grasp, swinging her hand high to keep the weapon out of the frenzied woman's reach.

'Got you!' a male voice snarled suddenly in her ear.

Rosie turned around. A red-faced policeman held her arm in a tight grip. With a swift movement, he jerked her arm around her back, hauling her off balance. As she fell, her head banged on to the back of one of the seats, sending her senses reeling. She landed awkwardly, her arm still twisted behind her. Unceremoniously, the policeman hauled her to her feet. Even as he held her, someone pulled at her hair. Rosie screamed and struggled to free herself but the police officer's grip was too strong for her.

'I've done nothing wrong,' she insisted. 'A woman was attacking me.'

'I don't see any other woman nearby,' the officer said curtly, 'and you stabbed me with that implement still in your hand.'

He now had both of her arms twisted behind her back.

‘Follow me outside,’ the officer commanded.

He began to force his way backwards through the scuffling that was still going on, dragging Rosie with him. She had no chance of keeping on her feet. Her whole body was wracked with pain. It seemed as though everyone she was dragged past took the opportunity to punch or kick her.

‘Let . . . me . . . walk!’ she implored in short gasps of breath.

She needn’t have bothered. Her feet were now shoeless and her heels were raw. The backs of her legs were scraped over the entrance threshold and she was dragged unceremoniously down the steps. Two other police officers grasped hold of her ankles and she was swung into the back of a police wagon.

‘That’s yer lot!’ her captor shouted to the driver. ‘Take ’em away!’

‘Rosie!’

As the wagon was jerked into action, Rosie couldn’t be sure, but she felt she heard her name shouted above the din.

It didn't really matter. There was nothing anyone could do to help her.

But Rosie hadn't been mistaken. Her name had been shouted. It was Sam.

He hadn't seen her since a few days earlier when Betty Draper had met him outside the works' gates to take him to his new digs. He later berated himself for not running after Rosie as he had longed to do. He hadn't been as uncaring as Rosie had thought him to be and had taken their separation badly. Try as he might to forget about her, he couldn't. The girls who were now almost throwing themselves at him weren't a patch on his Rosie and he longed to win Rosie back.

He knew she wouldn't back down, so the only thing to do, he had decided, was to study everything he could find about the emancipation of women — their aims, their ideals, their policies, their actions and the consequences they were prepared to face in the pursuit of their goal.

Knowing that Rosie was no longer at

the Bolton library, he spent his out-of-work hours over the next few days in the reading-room there. He emerged from his studies a changed man. Life, it seemed, was stacked against females from the moment they came into the world. The poorer the woman, the greater the prejudices were stacked against her. Men made the laws, with men in mind. All along the line, men were the beneficiaries of the unequal legal and social systems.

He was appalled by what he read. Things that Rosie had told him, implored him to listen to, he now saw for himself. Why had no-one in power learned the lessons from experience? Were all politicians mindful only of their own job? Were they afraid of being displaced if women had equal rights? What sort of government did that make them out to be?

He saw the advertisement for a meeting in Farnworth. A politician was to be the speaker. Sam had a few questions he would like to ask! He had listened to Mr Barnsley's speech with some derision. No wonder Rosie and her comrades had decided to take the fight for suffrage into their own hands, if this man was a true specimen of those in power.

Biding his time, he listened with interest to the opening questions and was just beginning to think most of them were a waste of breath when Rosie got to her feet. He couldn't take his eyes off her. As she hurled out her second question, his admiration of her grew. He wanted to stand up and declare to any who would listen that she was his girl and wasn't she grand? Then he mournfully admitted to himself she was no longer his girl, and he had only himself and his high-handed attitude to blame for that.

Sam was one of the first to rise to his feet at the end of her second question, intent on showing his approval. He led the initial cheers, his enthusiasm changing to alarm as the fracas began. Then he was swept along in the crush, at first away from the platform and almost flattened against the back wall. He saw the police enter the hall, truncheons flailing against more female heads than male, he noticed.

Sam began to fight his way forward towards the spot where Rosie had been standing. At first, he couldn't see her. He then noticed the man he had seen accompanying Rosie on Churchgate, Howard, he thought, saying something to a young woman. His eyes kept flickering away somewhere and when Sam followed his line of vision, he realised that the man was talking about Rosie. As he watched, the young woman began to push her way through the crowd towards Rosie. He saw her hand rise up and stab downwards. Because he was watching Rosie, he saw rather than heard her scream and he immediately began to hurl people out of his way as he tried to reach her side.

A surge of people forced him backwards again. Head and shoulders above most of the men, he saw Rosie struggle with the policeman and, with a roar that startled those around him, he surged forward. But for another tussle that ended at his feet, he might have reached her before she was hauled from the hall. As it was, he could only struggle helplessly to free himself from the tangle around him as he saw the policeman drag her almost inert form outside. Enraged, he flung himself forward again. He emerged into the night air in time to see the policeman bundle her into a police wagon.

He didn't know he had shouted her name. All he knew was a blind anger at the officer who had treated Rosie in such an unnecessary coarse fashion. As the wagon lurched into movement, Sam flung himself forward, intending to vent his anger on the police officer. Once more held back by the crowd, he suddenly saw Howard again. He flung himself at him and took him to the ground. For some reason known only to himself, this young man had instigated an incident to get Rosie into trouble and Sam wanted to know the reason why.

'I saw you, you rotter!' Sam shouted. 'I saw you! What's your game?'

Howard tried to push Sam's hands away.

'I don't know what you mean!' he gasped. 'Get off me, will you?'

Someone fell against Sam, dislodging his balance and Howard managed to twist his body around from under him. Sam didn't let go and the two men rolled over and over. Other men joined in and soon feet and fists collided with heads and bodies, no-one knowing who was fighting whom or for what reason they were fighting.

Eventually, Sam was hauled to his feet by three police officers. Partly dazed from his exertions, he could put up only a token resistance before he, too, was manacled and bundled into an already-crowded police wagon.

10

Rosie and the other women in the police wagon were so distressed by their short journey that they had no resistance left in them when the wagon eventually came to a halt. They were shepherded roughly into a huge, dark building. The dreadful sound as the door clanged shut behind them seemed to herald the start of a nightmare.

It was everything Annie had told her about — and more. Names and addresses were taken, from those who chose to give them. All were given a number and commanded to file into the next room. Here, they suffered the indignity of being searched for hidden weapons and all hairpins, brooches and other jewellery were taken from them and placed into paper bags bearing their name, if given, and a number.

They were then directed through

another door and herded down a bare corridor. The line moved on, towards what Rosie soon realised were the cells. At each door, they stopped whilst the officer in charge referred to a list of each cell's inmates and counted off the appropriate number of newcomers. Rosie and the woman behind her were directed into the second cell. It already had four occupants, and from their coarse comments, Rosie gathered they weren't too pleased to have two more cellmates.

The lighting was very dim. Rosie could just about make out that there were six bunks in two layers, two to each of the three inner walls. A folded blanket was at one end of each bunk. A bucket was situated in the far left-hand corner. It didn't need too many guesses to determine its use.

'Get your beds made. It's lights out in two minutes,' the officer commanded. 'And no talking!'

With no more ado, the door was closed with a resounding bang.

'Yer up on top,' a voice in the dimness told them. 'There, and there. And watch where yer put yer feet when yer climb up!'

A loud bell rang and the lights went out immediately. Rosie's companion squealed and clutched her arm.

'I can't see!'

'Silence!' a voice commanded through the grille.

They stumbled around in the darkness, and eventually scrambled up on to the higher bunks. The thin blanket gave scant comfort, and Rosie was glad it wasn't the middle of winter. Even so, it was cold in the cell, cold dark and smelly. It was a long, scary night. Rosie wondered if her father had been informed of her whereabouts and, if not, what he was thinking? Would he send Fred looking for her? She hadn't told them where she was going, knowing they might stop her.

The other girl was crying softly.

'Shut up!' a voice bade her.

The sobs became muffled. Rosie was scared, too. No-one had told them anything or shown them any compassion. She felt dirty and cold and her mind was far too active for sleep to come easily. She lay for a long time going over the evening's events.

She must have fallen asleep eventually, but it seemed as though it was only a few minutes later when a clanging bell summoned everyone to attention.

'Fold yer blanket and line up at door. One o' yer carry slop buckets!' an inmate told them.

Their door was unlocked and they filed silently into the corridor, joining on with the rest of the prisoners. Breakfast was served from a large cauldron of lumpy porridge, in a dull, cold hall. Each prisoner picked up a bowl and filed to a long trestle table and bench. They had to stand, holding their bowl until the table was filled.

'Sit!'

They all sat, but by then, the

porridge was nearly cold and completely tasteless. Rosie wrinkled her nose at it.

As soon as the meagre meal was over, they were herded out to the exercise yard, where they were made to parade around the edge of the yard in single file, speech strictly forbidden. A whistle was blown.

'Last night's batch line up by the door!'

As they filed through the door and spoke their number, they were sent to the left or the right. Rosie realised that all the ones from the meeting had been sent to the same side as she was. They were herded into a large room and lined up numerically.

'A magistrate comes now,' an old-hand whispered. 'Saves 'em sending us to 'im!'

She was correct. One by one they were ushered through the door. None returned. When it was Rosie's turn, she stepped forward fearfully. Nothing of what had been told them at the various meetings had given any preparation for this. For young women who had been law-abiding all their lives until recently, the whole procedure was a complete shock to them.

Rosie stepped into a small room. A stern-faced man sat at a table, a clerk at his side. The accompanying officer gripped Rosie's arm tightly.

'Name?'

'Rosie Mather.'

'How do you plead?'

Rosie swallowed.

'To what charge?' her voice croaked.

'Grievous bodily harm to a police officer in the course of his duty.'

'That is ridiculous! I did nothing, except try to defend myself!'

'Do you plead guilty or not guilty?'

'Not guilty, of course.'

'What is the evidence against this person?'

'A signed statement by an independent witness, sir.'

'Right. Guilty as charged. Prison for fourteen days. Next!'

Rosie was hustled out, her protests ignored.

'You'll keep your mouth shut, if you know what's good for you,' her accompanying officer snapped.

She was hustled into another room, where other women were standing in line, handcuffed like herself. Three officers paced up and down the lengthening line, insisting on absolute silence. Eventually, the outer door opened and they stepped briefly into the sunshine and then straight into a police wagon. It held eight of them. All were women who had been at the debate and apprehended in the rioting afterwards.

It was an uncomfortable ride. They were still under a command of silence, enforced by the two officers seated by the locked doors. Rosie found the lack of communication to be the hardest thing to bear. She realised that keeping them in ignorance of what was happening was part of the punishment. When they eventually arrived at their destination and were ordered out of the wagon, one prisoner risked further punishment by stating, 'It's Manchester.'

'Silence!'

Rosie glanced around. It was a bleak place. They were in a cobbled courtyard, surrounded on all four sides by a high, stone building with small, narrow windows. The small patch of blue sky, far above them, was the only bright colour to be seen.

Their treatment here was far worse than at the local police station. They were marched past a heavy, wooden door into a cold, stark building, and along a featureless corridor. Halfway along, they were commanded to turn left into a stone-flagged room, bare of any comforts. A wooden table stood in the middle and a rough wooden bench ran alongside two of the walls, with paper bags placed at regular intervals. Along the other wall was another long table with piles of clothes on it. At the far end, near the only other door, was a high desk.

Rosie rubbed at her wrists when the manacles were removed. Angry red marks remained to show where they had been.

'Prisoners, stand still!' a stern-faced woman sitting on a high stool at the front barked.

A poke in Rosie's back informed her that the command was issued to her. She was only easing her wrists.

'Eyes to the front!'

She decided to be prudent and obey the command.

'Prisoners, stand by a paper bag and strip. Place your clothes on top of the paper bag.'

Rosie hesitated and exchanged glances with her companions. A number of them, like herself, looking uncertain how to proceed.

'I said, strip!' the woman officer shouted.

'Here?' Rosie queried.

'I don't see any other place to go,' the officer snapped. 'Get on with it.'

An older woman, who seemed less startled, nudged Rosie.

'Just do it, love. It's part of their humiliation routine, under the guise of making sure we've no hatchets or such hidden under our skirts.'

'Silence! Any speaking among the prisoners will be punished.'

They were directed to the long table where an assortment of prison uniforms was spread. A prison orderly stood by each pile and handed a garment to each new prisoner as they filed past — calico drawers; a thick green calico skirt decorated with black arrows that looked as though it hadn't been washed in months; a shapeless shirt, again decorated with black arrows; a checked pinafore; a prison mobcap with tapes to tie under the chin; a pair of rough woollen socks, and a pair of large boots.

Most of the women were now shivering with a mixture of fear and cold. They pulled on the unfamiliar garments, adjusting the width of the skirts and shirts with tapes around their waist. The socks were itchy and the boots were far too large for most of them but complaints merely earned a sharp reprimand from the officer-in-charge.

The line of ill-clad prisoners processed into the next room, where they were given a bible, a hymn book, a book of rules and pair of thin sheets. Many of the women were weeping by now and Rosie felt bowed under the dark oppression of the place.

The days that followed merged into a long, dark nightmare from which there seemed no end. After four days of suffering gibes and insults from other prisoners, abetted by unsympathetic warders, poor food and humiliating practices, four of Rosie's group decided that, in for a penny, in for a pound, they would go on hunger strike to highlight the appalling conditions of their imprisonment.

Rosie was one of them.

The four protesters were isolated from any contact other than that of their warders. For five days, their food was brought to them and later removed, untouched. A cup of water was all they had agreed to partake of each meal-time. Rosie knew she was growing weaker. Her limbs were shaky; her hair hung lankly around her face; her scalp itched. She felt dirty and unkempt, but her resolution remained strong. Surely they must give in and grant her an audience with the governor.

Night and day, already confused by the perpetual dimness inside the prison, became meaningless. Hallucinations merged with the living nightmare and Rosie couldn't differentiate between the two. The warder's face loomed and receded. Her father was there, shouting in anger but whether for or against her, she couldn't determine. Of Fred there was no doubt where his anger lay, and there was Sam.

The sweetness of his face brought comfort to her heart. Oh, how she loved him! Sam! Forgive me! Where are you, Sam? Have you missed me? Do you still love me? Then she remembered — she had lost him. Her world sank into total blackness.

On her tenth day of imprisonment, a grim-faced warder opened Rosie's cell door.

'Get up!' she commanded.

'What was that?' Rosie stammered, her lips swollen and her throat too sore to allow her to swallow.

'Get up and follow me!'

Rosie pushed herself upright on her pallet. The cell door was open. She must have heard aright. She slowly pulled herself to her feet and put out a hand against the wall to steady herself. As she tried to pass through the doorway, she stumbled against the warder. The warder gripped her arm in a fist of steel and pushed her roughly against the doorjamb.

'Try that again an' yer'll be on a charge.'

'Where am I going?'

'Yer'll find out!'

When the cell stopped spinning

around, Rosie allowed the warder to hustle her out of the cell and along the dim corridor, her legs threatening to collapse at the knees. Only the grip of steel around her arm kept her at the warder's side.

It seemed a long way to the end of the corridor.

At a curt nod, a metal grilled door was opened, as were the following three. In a stark room that seemed vaguely familiar, a paper packet was thrust at Rosie.

'Put on your clothes,' she was ordered.

Rosie's trembling hands tore at the tapes and fastenings of her prison garb and she changed into her own clothes. They felt far too large. As she dressed, the door was opened three times and the three other hunger-strikers were hustled one by one into the room. All looked as bewildered as Rosie felt.

'Follow me!'

The releasing officer strode off again and the four women tremulously followed her, hardly daring to believe that they were being released. How long had it been? Had they completed their sentence? Rosie didn't know.

It was dark in the last corridor, until the door was opened, letting in the blinding light from outside. There was a cobbled yard and, at the far end, another doorway. It seemed a mile away! Rosie felt her legs wouldn't have the strength to carry her there, but they did.

Blinking rapidly, Rosie stepped through the door. The sound of cheering greeted her and a small group of people ran forward, calling out their various names. Everyone wanted to shake their hands or clap them on their backs. Howard was there, taking photographs, and Annie. Mildred Leatherbarrow was also there and many others, but not the one Rosie wanted to see.

Sam wasn't there.

Disappointment flooded her. He didn't love her. He didn't want her back.

'Now, you're coming home with me, Rosie,' Mildred informed her. 'I've settled it with your father and he agrees that it is for the best.'

Rosie was devastated. She looked at her tearfully.

'Doesn't he want me?'

'It's nothing like that. Well, it's your brother and his wife. They . . . '

'His wife?' Rosie exclaimed. 'Fred isn't married.'

'He is now. They . . . er . . . thought it best, so that Edith could take care of your father,' Mildred tried to explain. 'And it seems that Edith isn't yet ready to let you into her house. I'm sorry, Rosie. I'm sure she'll come round. Anyway,' she added briskly, 'you'll be quite comfortable with me for the time being, so, come on. We've got transport for you.'

Rosie felt weepy. She was pleased to be out of prison but just wanted to get away somewhere quiet to come to terms with her release and the fact that she have been cast out of her own home. Mildred understood. These weren't the first young women she had met coming out of prison. She turned to the others.

'That's it for now, everyone. These ladies need some rest and building up. I'll keep you all informed. No, not even you, Mr Baxter. Off you go, now.'

'Write about it, Rosie,' Howard shouted to her. 'Do it now, while everything is fresh in your mind. I'll get it in the newspaper.'

Rosie barely took it in. She was thankful to be swept along in Mildred Leatherbarrow's care. She was given a small drink of milk, a hot bath and tucked up into a warm bed. Later, she had some milk-soaked bread, followed by a full night's sleep. Mildred kept her in seclusion for three days, guarding her from the outside world and, afterwards, carefully monitored any visitors, staying in the room with Rosie and timing any visits.

As Rosie's strength returned, she recalled Howard's shouted instruction to her and she began to jot down her memories of her imprisonment, trying to keep everything factual, rather than over-dramatic. By the time Howard was allowed in to see her, the article was nearly ready.

'I'll bring it to you as soon as I've finished it,' Rosie promised him. 'I'm ready to go out again. It will do me good.'

'Are you also ready to become my girl?'

Rosie's smile faded. She knew she still loved Sam. It wouldn't be fair to go out with anyone until she had got Sam out of her system.

'I'm sorry, Howard. I like you, but it's not enough, is it?'

'You might learn to love me in time,' Howard said hopefully.

Rosie shook her head. She couldn't imagine ever loving anyone else like she loved Sam. She touched his arm gently.

'Maybe, but not for a long time. We can still be friends, though, can't we? I'd be sorry to lose your friendship.'

As Howard rose to go, he managed a rueful smile.

'I suppose so. Anyway, hurry up with your article. My editor is keen to see it.'

Rosie felt unsettled after he had left. Had she done the right thing? She thought so. She didn't want to settle for second-best and if Sam no longer wanted her, then she would fling herself into her work and use her energies to forward the women's cause, for the foreseeable future at least.

Her first outside visit was to see her father. A little apprehensively, she turned into the top of their street. The sight of Betty Draper only a few yards away did nothing to improve her morale. She stopped abruptly. Was she still seeing Sam? The very thought hurt. Her throat felt tight but she had to ask.

'Hello, Betty.'

Betty tossed back her head and made an audible sniff. She made as though to push past Rosie without speaking, but Rosie reached out a hand and touched her arm.

‘How’s Sam?’ Rosie faltered.

‘What’s that to you?’ Betty scorned, shaking off her hand,.

‘I’ve been . . . away. I just wondered,’ Rosie made herself say.

‘Huh! Well, he’s not been wondering about you! Nob’dy’ll want yer now, jailbird, not even yer own dad!’

Rosie felt nothing but contempt for her.

‘I’m not ashamed of being in prison. It was for a worthy cause. I would like to see Sam. Do you know where he’s living now?’

It cost her a lot to ask the question but she couldn’t just believe that their love had ended. She had to see him, ask his forgiveness for her high-handed attitude towards him and his less liberal views. Surely they could compromise their views and live in harmony. Others did so.

Betty smiled coldly.

‘I finished with ’im, if you must know, and he’s gone away.’

‘Gone away? Where to?’

'How should I know? I'm not in the least bit interested!'

With that, Betty departed, leaving a devastated Rosie staring after her. So, it was over. He'd have waited until she had been released if he still cared about her. She'd have to accept it, however hard it was. She felt knocked sideways, though. She had convinced herself that they could be reconciled.

With a deep sigh, she made her way down the street. The door would be on the latch, she knew. Her brother's new wife, Edith, was standing at the sink, up to her elbows in suds. When Edith saw who their visitor was, she immediately reached for a towel and moved to block her way.

'This is my house now, and yer not welcome.'

Rosie ignored her words and pushed her way past.

'You might regard this as your home now, Edith,' she said quietly, 'but I'm coming in to see Dad, even if I have to knock you out of the way.'

'Well, that's all yer fit for, isn't it?'

'Leave it off, Edith,' Alf spoke from his fireside chair. 'I'll see my daughter, if you don't mind.'

Rosie hugged him and he said he was pleased to see her but the atmosphere was strained. Rosie didn't stay long. She knew it was useless to return to live there until she was strong enough to stand on her feet against Edith, and Fred's scathing comments about her prison sentence. She promised to return in a few days.

It was Howard who eventually told her the truth about Sam, when she took her finished article to him at the newspaper offices.

'I met your boyfriend,' he said lightly.

Rosie froze.

'I haven't got a boyfriend,' she said coldly, trying not to let her memories of Sam spring into her mind.

'He seemed pretty desperate to rush to your rescue then.'

'I don't know what you mean.'

'The night you were arrested. We

. . . er . . . sort of bumped into each other.'

Rosie was puzzled.

'When?'

'At the meeting.'

'The meeting? He was there?'

'Yes, quite voluble in your defence. He's due out tomorrow,' he added.

'Due out? Out from where?'

'Prison, my love! You aren't the only one with a police record, you know!'

Rosie stared at Howard, aghast.

'Prison? Sam? Are you sure?'

Howard rubbed his chin.

'He got into a fight, and nearly wrecked the remand centre he was taken to, trying to get out. He seemed to think he could rescue you from the women's prison single-handed. Got his sentence doubled, I'm afraid.'

The full meaning of Howard's words suddenly cleared her mind. Rosie narrowed her eyes.

'Why didn't you tell me this before? You must have known I would want to know.'

Howard grimaced.

'I'm sorry. I kept hoping you might transfer your affections to me. All's fair in love and war, and all that. But I've now accepted we're just friends, so I thought I'd better come clean.' He grinned at her. 'It would be a shame to spoil a lovely friendship, wouldn't it?'

'Huh! Some friendship! I don't know how you have the gall to stand there grinning at me.'

Her initial anger was fading, allowing her brain to slip into gear.

'Which prison is Sam in, and what time is he due out?'

'He's at Manchester, not far from where you were. His release time is nine o'clock tomorrow morning.'

'What? You've left it a bit late, haven't you? I must be there. You'll have to help me.'

'Can't do, I'm afraid. I'll be at work.'

Rosie grabbed back her manuscript and held it high, out of Howard's reach.

'What's it worth?' she threatened, beginning to tear it in two.

'You wouldn't!'

'I would!'

'I'll see my boss.'

So it was, at nine o'clock the following morning, Rosie was standing outside the prison, her hands clasped together as the minutes ticked by. There was no welcoming crowd, such as received her, only Rosie and Howard.

'You're sure you got the day and time right?' she asked Howard anxiously for the umpteenth time.

She was nervous, that's what it was. What if Sam no longer cared for her, no longer wanted her? How would she bear it?

'They don't stand waiting with a stopwatch, you know.'

'No, but . . . '

Her voice broke off as the small door in the huge prison gates opened and a lonely figure stepped through.

'Sam!'

She hadn't meant to call his name. It slipped unbidden from her lips. Her hand flew to her mouth, her fingers spread across her lips as she paused uncertainly. Sam stood still, blinking his eyes as the brightness of the open air lit upon him, a slow smile spreading across his face. His whole attention was now focused on Rosie's face and he began to move forward.

With a cry, Rosie sped towards him. He held his arms wide and Rosie flew into them.

'I was afraid you no longer loved me!' Rosie almost sobbed, laughing and crying at the same time.

Sam swung her around and then lowered her feet to the ground. He gazed solemnly into her eyes.

'I love the very heart of you, Rosie Mather!'

He pulled her to him and kissed her as though he never meant to let her go, which he didn't, of course!

'I'm sorry I was slow to support you,' he said at last.

'I'm sorry I aggravated you so much!'

'Does that mean you're ready to obey my every word?'

Rosie stepped back and looked at him quizzically.

'I shouldn't think so!'

Sam grinned.

'Then it's as well we've got a lifetime to sort ourselves out, isn't it?'

Rosie tucked her hand into his arm and cuddled into his side.

'Yes, and the sooner we start, the better!'

THE END

Other titles in the
Linford Romance Library:

CONVALESCENT HEART

Lynne Collins

They called Romily the Snow Queen, but once she had been all fire and passion, kindled into loving by a man's kiss and sure it would last a lifetime. She still believed it would, for her. It had lasted only a few months for the man who had stormed into her heart. After Greg, how could she trust any man again? So was it likely that surgeon Jake Conway could pierce the icy armour that the lovely ward sister had wrapped about her emotions?

TOO MANY LOVES

Juliet Gray

Justin Caldwell, a famous personality of stage and screen, was blessed with good looks and charm that few women could resist. Stacy was a newcomer to England and she was not impressed by the handsome stranger; she thought him arrogant, ill-mannered and detestable. By the time that Justin desired to begin again on a new footing it was much too late to redeem himself in her eyes, for there had been too many loves in his life.

MYSTERY AT MELBECK

Gillian Kaye

Meg Bowering goes to Melbeck House in the Yorkshire Dales to nurse the rich, elderly Mrs Peacock. She likes her patient and is immediately attracted to Mrs Peacock's nephew and heir, Geoffrey, who farms nearby. But Geoffrey is a gambling man and Meg could never have foreseen the dreadful chain of events which follow. Throughout her ordeal, she is helped by the local vicar, Andrew Sheratt, and she soon discovers where her heart really lies.